NEFARIOUS

D. SEAN

This book is a work of fiction. Names, characters, places and incidents are products of the author's imagination or are used fictitiously. Any resemblance to actual events or locales or persons, living or dead, is entirely coincidental.

Copyright © 2015 by D. Sean

DSEANBOOKS.COM

RAINDUST LLC
P. O. Box 669281
Marietta, GA 30066
raindustllc.com
Published by Raindust LLC

ISBN-13: 978-0-9834034-7-0
ISBN-10: 0983403473
Sean, D. Nefarious/ by D. Sean

Dude

PROLOGUE

Cavanaugh rolled to his side, still asleep for the most part. He felt the hardwood beneath his body, which meant he'd never moved from the floor and, as a consequence, had slept there. It wasn't the first time it'd happened, and he would wager a hefty bet it would not be the last. He groped for the softness of Sarah among the hard surface without parting his eyelids.

"Seej?" he called into the quiet but received no answer.

This little name he'd given Sarah was a combination of initials. He often teased her about them with lame jokes that riddled him with laughter. Him and no one else. Her initials spelled the word "see." He'd added a "j" for Jones, therefore dubbing her Seej.

He continued to grope the cold, wet sheets where

he lay. Wait, why were they wet? Surely he hadn't pissed himself, or had he? He had not been that drunk since college. Perhaps that was the reason Sarah wasn't next to him where she should be. That still didn't explain the wetness...nor the stickiness.

Cavanaugh, his eyelids crusted together with the evidence of sleep, forced his eyes open. He needed to inspect what his fingers were touching. Taking the back of his hand, he rubbed one eye, trying to remove some of the goo so he could see. Opening his eyes in stages, he winced at the brightness of the sun as it washed the dark paint of his bedroom walls. Straining to focus on the pillow where Sarah should be laying, Cavanaugh cast his eyes downward expecting to see her wrapped in the tangle of sheets. His breath caught on an inhale.

"Wha—?" His voice came out in a low whisper, scratchy and thick.

In a frantic flail of hands and feet, Cavanaugh pushed the sheets away from him. He wrestled with the covers that blanketed him, trying to extract himself, all the while sliding backwards on the floor, away from the horrific vision he hoped was a nightmare. Could he still be asleep? He hoped to God he was. Although he'd never believed in all that holy mumbo jumbo, if any of it were true, he didn't want to dismiss it now. *God, please let me be dreaming*, he thought, not wanting to hear his own voice again.

He kept sliding for what felt like an infinite distance until his back slammed into a bookcase against the wall. The shelves, filled with Sarah's girlie magazines, notebooks, and puzzles banged and rattled, shaking its books loose from their perches. One of her beloved puzzle books fell beside Cavanaugh as he stared, mouth agape, at the vision that it seemed he wasn't going to wake up from.

The pastel colored, floral sheets had been saturated, stained a sickening shade of red, while the smell of iron permeated the air. In his effort to flee—a feeble attempt, at best—Cavanaugh had streaked the substance across the floor where it ended on the spot where he sat. He looked around in confusion and disbelief, wondering where the blood had come from.

Cavanaugh did a vague body check on himself, patting his chest, thighs and arms, pretty certain the blood wasn't his. If it were his, if he'd been injured, he'd, without question, feel some type of pain. He would have to for the amount of blood on the sheets and floor. His stomach twisted and churned at his next thought. The grimmest possibility seemed the one explanation. His nausea swelled, expanding inside his belly until brimming on the verge of making him heave. He could aid a birthing colt without getting squeamish but the sight of human blood sickened him. Where had the blood come from? It hadn't come from him, and the only other person who'd been there, the other person who'd been in the apartment with him...

"Sarah!" he yelled. Sheer panic made his voice

sound octaves higher than normal. "Seej? Where are you?"

Cavanaugh yanked himself free of the soiled sheets and jumped to his feet, standing in his underwear and socks. His pants, along with a pair of his favorite cowboy boots, had been tossed aside and now soaked up the blood in the corner of the room. He looked down at his stained body. What the hell had happened?

Cavanaugh padded around the small apartment, looking for Sarah in each room, until he made his way back to their bedroom. He stared at the blood, and unable to stifle it any longer, raced to the bathroom and retched into the sink. Though just a couple feet away, the toilet proved too far.

As Cavanaugh clutched either side of the basin, he raised his eyes to the mirror. Examining his reflection, something in his eyes didn't look familiar. A tiny smirk formed at the corner of his mouth, showing itself for a fraction of a second before it disappeared. It came and went so fast that Cavanaugh couldn't be certain if he'd seen it at all. Waking up in a pool of blood wasn't the least bit amusing, in particular when you suspected it might be that of someone you love. He watched his face in the mirror, changing angles, waiting to see if the tiny smile would show itself again, as if he had no control over his facial functions.

At a point, Cavanaugh pulled his eyes from the mirror and looked down at himself, his body a bloody canvas, a spattered, macabre image. The vision sent him into a frenzy. He clawed at his skin as though the red streaks were layers of hydraulic acid. He spun in circles trying to reach every spot where the blood stained him, attacking his thighs with a vigorous, almost vengeful rubbing, which smeared the blood on the places it had not already covered. This made him more frantic, more erratic.

"Fuck!"

Cavanaugh, mid-spin, had rammed his hip into the sink and had fallen backwards into the shower, tearing links of the shower curtain from the hooks. Without thinking, he turned on the closest tap. The water came in a cold rush, and Cavanaugh wished it would be the agent that would, at last, wake him. This "nightmare" gave him an intense longing for complete sobriety, something he could never remember wanting. Besides that, he couldn't stomach the stench and sight of the blood, and he feared he'd vomit again and again until he was either free from it or had fled it. He turned his back as the colored water swirled down the drain, scrubbing and scratching his skin until it, at least, looked clean, since he didn't feel clean at all.

Cavanaugh dusted a dry towel over his body when he exited the shower, then used it to pick up an armful of the soiled sheets, dumping them into the tub where he'd left the water running. He yanked the curtain closed as much as it would allow, hoping that would wash away the reality, but knowing it wouldn't.

After standing there for a moment, Cavanaugh exited the bathroom and haphazardly threw on a pair of crumpled jeans that lay across a wicker chair. He grabbed the first shirt he could find, fighting with the armholes as he tried to get it on and then jammed his feet into a pair of unstained boots and headed for the door. Cavanaugh had his hand extended for the doorknob when he heard a crunch beneath his foot. When he lifted it, he saw Sarah's favorite pair of glasses. A pair of battered frames and now crushed lenses. Still amid his panic, Cavanaugh thought of how pissed she would be.

"Shit." He sighed, shaking his head, thinking of the lashing she'd give him.

He swept up the fragments into his large hands and dropped them onto the breakfast bar. Before he walked out the door, he took another glance at their bedroom. The mattress was bare, save for one lone pillow, rumpled and dented at the foot of the bed. The pillowcase, half off, revealed the stained fabric beneath. He stood there for a long moment, dazed, staring at the room until he heard the bray of a horse, snapping him out of his trance. He dashed out the door, making a run for the stalls.

CHAPTER ONE

"Sally! Come on!"

"My name is SARAH! You asshole!"

"Well, since you know your name, why don't you just make time and get your ass over here?"

Cavanaugh spoke in a slow drawl. His speech, already somewhat distorted by his heavy Texan accent, became more indistinguishable by his slur. His words were as drunk as he was. Every one that came out of his throat lost its momentum by the time it made it to his lips. Syllables overlapped and pronunciations crashed into one another because of the bourbon, scotch, and whiskey he had been drinking. The combination of all three needed no more than the strike of a match to explode, or in his case, implode. Sarah, or Sally, as he called her tonight was that spark of fire.

Sarah Evans and Cavanaugh had been together for well over two years, but he often got her name wrong. Tonight proved to be a good night because at least her name started with an "S," as close to right as he'd get. Sarah trailed behind him, the rage filling the space between them. A diminutive five feet, one inch tall, Sarah had a tiny figure. Her dirty blond hair, dark at the roots and tapered at the neck, lay coiffed, in near perfect condition, notwithstanding hours of Cavanaugh ruffling it. Her purple-rimmed glasses balanced on the bridge of her nose, ill-fitting and warped. Despite having contacts, she preferred the shabby spectacles. Pushing them up on her nose for the third time, she continued to follow behind Cavanaugh.

Sarah had a hard time balancing herself on her red suede stilettos as she traipsed through the graveled parking lot to Cavanaugh's car. Her foot kept slipping to the side, threatening to sprain her ankle, if not break it. Cavanaugh turned around, sloshing his near empty glass of dark liquor onto the sleeve of his tan blazer, his movements exaggerated. He took a breath to yell at her again.

"Shut up! I said I'm comin'!" Sarah said, not giving the slow moving words in his head the chance to come out of his mouth.

He muttered something Sarah couldn't understand. She doubted he knew what he'd said, even to himself. Of course, that made no difference. He raised the pilfered glass and gulped down the remainder of his drink, licking his lips afterwards. He peered into the glass as though it would somehow refill itself if he stared long enough. After a minute, he seemed to come to terms with the fact that it wouldn't and smashed the lowball glass to the ground. A spray of glass shards flew in various directions, one of which whizzed by Sarah's face, missing her flushed cheek by the narrowest of margins. Another speck nicked the top of her foot, causing her to stumble more.

"Son of a bi—! Dammit, Cav! You're such an idiot, God! That glass—Ugh!" Sarah, so furious, couldn't finish more than one sentence.

"Watch out, San, there's glass on the ground," he warned, staggering sideways.

"No shit." Sarah looked down at the bleeding cut on her foot.

Too unstable to do more than take a moment to look at the cut, Sarah side-stepped the crash site and made her way to Cavanaugh's side. She arrived just in time to keep him from falling to the ground. Sarah worked to keep them both upright. If she hit the ground too, she'd have bloody knees to match her foot considering her cut-off jeans left her legs exposed from ankle to upper thighs.

"I love you, Shelly." Cavanaugh spoke into the side of her face, planting a wet, odorous kiss at the corner of her mouth.

He leaned the bulk of his five foot, nine inch frame onto her shoulders, the same shoulders that struggled to carry a heavy backpack, let alone support over a hundred extra pounds. She struggled to keep her footing but managed to shove him upwards and regain some stability.

"I'm sure Shelly loves you too, you drunk bastard."

Sarah wanted to call him another name...Jeff, Dick, Sam, Dumbass, but she dared not. The last time she'd done that, it cost her. Cavanaugh had gone into a rage she never wanted to see again. He had screamed at her, nose to nose, and punched her so hard in the stomach that she vomited right then...all over him. His weak stomach became her saving grace. The sight and smell of the rancid contents caused him to vomit too. She could curse him at will and call him names, but the names of other men, fictional or otherwise, sent him into a fury.

Cavanaugh half-walked, half-dragged himself forward while Sarah bore the brunt of his weight. Lucky for her, they were a few feet from the car and Sarah had the keys, having long ago extracted them from Cavanaugh's pocket. She knew where the night would end almost before it began, not that it ever changed.

Sarah didn't need the keys to drive them home. As

long as the key was near the car, she could get in and use the push button to start it. However, in Cavanaugh's mind, whoever held the keys would be the driver, no matter how inebriated. In knowing that, Sarah made sure to swipe them at the first opportunity. Cavanaugh drove a late model Lexus IS convertible with retractable roof, which he'd left lowered. The weather had favored them, holding off the rains. On a previous night, Sarah had found herself dashing outside to put the roof up, thanks to Cavanaugh's absentmindedness.

When they were close enough to the vehicle, as a minute gesture of revenge, Sarah pushed Cavanaugh the final foot onto the car. She snickered as she watched him flail his arms as if he were teetering on the edge of cliff. He fell against the car with a relieved sigh, his expression conveying that of someone who'd just escaped death. Sarah reached for the door handle, hearing the telltale beep which indicated the doors had unlocked. She pulled the door open while Cavanaugh began a lateral slide towards the ground. For a moment, Sarah contemplated letting him hit the rocky ground and choke on a mouth full of gravel, but thought better of it since she would be the one who'd have to pick his heavy ass up and try to get him into the car. She grabbed his arm to leverage him.

"Come on, Cav, get in," she mumbled more to herself than him, not that he'd been listening.

Sarah often called him Cav, a nickname she'd given

him, but he wasn't always receptive to it. Almost no one ever called him anything but Cavanaugh. He didn't like the nicknames given to him, including CJ, a moniker from his childhood which much of his family still called him.

With a grunt, Cavanaugh fell into the passenger seat and slumped onto the console. Sarah had to pick up each of his legs and cram them into the footwell. She didn't bother adjusting the seat; instead, she left it positioned for her small frame in lieu of making room for his long legs. He wouldn't notice the discomfort of his compressed knees until morning, if at all. She pulled the seat belt and leaned over him to fasten it. As she fumbled to snap the buckle into place, Cavanaugh took the opportunity to place his mouth over one of her adolescent-sized breasts, attempting to suckle it. He ended up with a mouth full of fabric but managed to dampen her plaid shirt right over her now distended nipple. Although Sarah ignored the gesture, her body did not. Cavanaugh laughed as she shut the door.

She made her way around to the driver's side of the vehicle. As she slid into the luxurious leather seat, she thanked her lucky stars that she had learned to drive a stick shift as a teenager. Despite not having driven one in years, she'd never forgotten how. Most girls she knew didn't have the knowledge or the desire to operate a manual transmission, but for her, it provided a level of freedom. The freedom to choose. She could choose any vehicle she wanted and not be limited by its features.

She felt privileged to drive a car like this, whether if by default or not. The vehicle had a 204 horsepower engine, went from zero to sixty in less than eight and a half seconds, and topped out at a speed of 134 miles per hour. The car cost more than she made in two years at any job she'd ever worked. Cavanaugh never seemed to trust her driving, although she wondered how he thought they made it home on nights like this one. He couldn't think himself capable enough to get them home unharmed, could he?

Sarah knew more about Cavanaugh's car than he did. She just about grew up in a repair shop, playing with tools instead of dolls, pretending to be a mechanic instead of a housewife and spending time under the hoods of cars instead of under the bleachers with boys.

Nestled in the seat, she strapped herself in and pressed one of the programmable buttons to adjust chair's position. She had, without Cavanaugh's knowledge, personalized one of them for herself, doubting he realized the feature existed, let alone that she'd converted one of them. Next, she pressed the button to start the car and looked over at Cavanaugh, already asleep with his mouth wide open, a trickle of drool dripping from the corner of his lips onto the console.

Sarah pulled out of the makeshift parking lot, listening as the gravel shifted and crunched beneath the tires. She stole another glance at the man she'd fallen in love with by accident and wondered how and why. She asked questions and answered them all in the same process of thought. As she turned her eyes back to the road, her mind wandered to the day she'd met the one and only Cavanaugh Jones.

CHAPTER TWO

Two years ago, on a warm day in the South, Sarah, made an effort to claim her freedom. She'd boarded a train headed west, hoping to plant new roots in sunny California. Wearing a pair of shorts, white halter-top and canvas sneakers, she'd crammed a hiker's backpack with clothes, shoes, and dreams, although the dreams tended to be a little fuzzy.

Sarah had been born in the small town of Beaufort, South Carolina. The entire city spanned less than twenty-five square miles, total. Not much of a city at all, a tour of Beaufort took less than thirty minutes. Sarah hadn't known anything outside of what her little town had to offer. All of her friends were Beaufort natives and all the schools she'd ever attended had Beaufort in the name.

Tired of the small town with all its small-minded

people, Sarah, had big dreams, despite not knowing what they were yet. However, she did know she wouldn't achieve her dreams in Beaufort. It seemed many celebrities had packed up on a whim and moved to California or New York to live the life they'd fantasized about. Why couldn't she? With that in mind, she'd chosen California over New York, whose winters were much colder than Sarah assumed she could tolerate. Growing up in the South had given her an affinity for warm weather, so she made the obvious choice. Sarah's best friend, Taylor-Lynn, the sole person who knew about her plans, had become her accomplice and took her to the bus station.

Sarah, the only child of her father and the eldest of two from her mother, didn't know much about the woman who'd birthed her, apart from her name and a vague recollection of her face. Elaine Page, who had never taken her married name, fled Beaufort before Sarah turned five years old, already pregnant with another man's baby. Whether by force or choice Sarah never knew, but either way she felt abandoned, left to raise her father or could it have been the other way around? She could never be sure. She'd always felt a responsibility to pick up the pieces of his crumbled life that her mother had left, even at five years old.

The bus ride to Los Angeles would take almost three days, but that's what she could afford. Sarah had saved the money she earned working at the local Walmart for two years. About half her check went towards groceries and household items that her father didn't have sense enough to buy: toiletries, cleaning supplies, food. He, a military retiree, had received an honorary discharge because of illness for which Sarah had always assumed to be that of a broken heart. With nothing for him to do and Sarah to take care of all the things he did not, it left him with one daily activity: drinking.

Not that Beaufort had an extensive list of pastimes. In fact, there was no list at all. The younger kids would hang out in the Walmart parking lot—the thing to do on a Saturday night. Sarah and her friends would spend most of their time on the beach, both day and night. That's one of the things she loved most about her hometown and why California became her destination of choice.

Sarah's friends had a difficult time understanding her desperation to leave the place they loved so much. They couldn't understand why, though she had a job, she never had any money. Sarah could see the invisible path to freedom, a constant motivation to shove dollar after dollar in various hiding places of her small room until she'd amassed enough money for a ticket out of Beaufort.

She'd managed to save a little over $2000, pay the utilities for the trailer she shared with her father three months in advance, and leave a few hundred dollars for him before leaving. She knew he wouldn't find it until she'd almost made it to California and by then it'd be too late to talk her out of it. Sarah also stocked up on toiletries and frozen food for him. As far as he knew, she'd gone to spend time with Taylor-Lynn's family in Hilton Head.

Sarah stepped off the Greyhound bus in Abilene, Texas, the twenty-third stop among the thirty-nine scheduled which included the final destination; she'd counted. It may not have been the most glamorous way to enter her field of dreams, but it had, for certain, been the cheapest. She had a thirty-minute layover in Abilene, and as she looked around trying to locate the restrooms, her eyes grazed over a stranger's profile. He talked with someone in a maintenance uniform, seeming to use his hands more than his mouth. He had broad shoulders, covered by an ochre-colored blazer and large hands with almost sausage-like fingers. His sandy brown hair, slicked back to the nape of his neck, complemented his clean-shaven face.

For an instant, he looked her way, but didn't seem to see her. Unable to ignore the urgency in her bladder any longer, Sarah found her way to the restrooms where she spent most of her layover. She groomed herself with moist towelettes and took the extra time to brush her teeth and hair. Just before she emerged, she misted herself with lavender-scented body spray. Although she didn't feel quite human, she didn't feel like an odorous monster anymore either.

During her survey of the station, she'd spotted a vending machine. Certain the snacks inside were near expiration if not already growing new organisms, she decided to get something anyway. Not that she had any other food choices. Putting her bill into the slot, she chose the snack with the lesser probability of transmitting disease.

"B, 4," Sarah said aloud as she pushed the buttons.

She watched with anticipation as the rings turned to release her crackers but they stopped just shy of the last quarter inch needed to drop.

"Really!" Sarah yelled at the machine and pulled her leg back to give it a quick kick. Before she could make contact, she heard:

"I wouldn't do that if I were you."

"Oh yeah, and what would you do?" The bold tone moved past her lips but she didn't take her eyes away from her coveted crackers.

"Well, Miss..." the man began but paused since he didn't have her name to fill in the blank. Sarah's eyes still had not moved. "Miss?" He leaned forward, dropping his head to the side.

At last, she turned and recognized the man in the blazer whom she'd spied earlier. Speechless, she stared at him. Having a closer view made what she'd seen from afar a bit of a joke. His shoulders looked wider up close and his chest spread from one end to the other, hefty and muscular. Most of his features were broad that way, including his nose and cheekbones. Sarah found his smile to be wide as well, spreading across the majority of his face. She also noticed premature wrinkles around his eyes and mouth, making her wonder about his age.

"Are you going to tell me your name?" he asked, his tone laced with impatience.

"Sarah," she answered, quick on the heels of his question. Too quick.

"Sarah? Just, Sarah? Like Elvis, Jewel...Garth? Wait, Garth goes by two names doesn't he?" The man laughed at himself. This solicited a giggle out of Sarah. "Wow, she smiles, ladies and gentlemen. We have ourselves a smile." As if trying to get a better view, he leaned back a little.

"My last name is Evans."

Sarah felt a bit self-conscious under the stranger's gaze. Most often, Sarah would be a lot more defensive, but she found herself disarmed by this man's presence yet, at the same time, unnerved by his effect on her.

"The pleasure is mine, Sarah Evans."

He spoke her name slowly, lacing it with charm

and an indecipherable innuendo. As the words spilled from his mouth like the dawdling drip from a leaking faucet, he tipped his imaginary hat to her, a gesture she found alluring. Each fell silent.

The stranger—who had not yet introduced himself—wondered why he felt enamored with this girl who, a minute ago, had been one kick away from damaging his property. He had never had difficulty with women... ever. Between his wealth, country boy good looks and the undulating charm which he had no desire to control, he'd had more than his fair share of women. Besides that, there were so many more he hadn't known. He'd just scratched the surface, but this one...

This young unsuspecting beauty, with what he guessed to be a vile temper and somewhat shy disposition, had an unseen advantage over him. Plowing straight into his heart, he couldn't ascertain the planes and avenues she traveled but he was a stubborn old stallion and determined then to find out. He needed to know why he felt such an instantaneous need to care for her, take care of her, cradle her, run his fingers through her hair. He needed to understand the feeling of already knowing her, as though this weren't the first time they'd met, but a convergence numbered in the thousands.

He felt a desperate need to both suppress and express this feeling forcing its way upward like rancid bile, before projectile vomiting. Having had the latter feeling before, he knew it well, but the rest, he hadn't felt anything like it before—at least, not like this. Of course, he cared for his parents, his friends, his horses, and his life, but caring for a woman meant trouble. Love changed people, and he had no desire for change. Unfortunately, he didn't seem to have any control or choice in the matter.

Still staring at her, his mind spun out of control. He thought of all the things he wanted to do for her and to her. His heart pumped with new blood, new life, and wild endorphins.

She moved then, shifting her miniature weight, bringing him back to the place where they stood. The noise rushed in on him like a freight train with near deafening sound. He became aware of the people around them, the buses, the time, but he felt most aware of her. He cleared his throat. Well, at least he tried.

"Cavanaugh...Jones."

The words tumbled from his mouth, clumsy and slow. Sarah made the slightest acknowledgement with her eyes indicating that she'd heard him. *How did I know that?* Cavanaugh thought. Such a minute expression would have been lost on anyone, should have been lost upon him as well. He may know a lot about women, but he wasn't that damned good.

Sarah had no idea what to say to him now. She kept repeating his name in her head: Cavanaugh Jones, Cavanaugh Jones...such an unusual name, but something about it made her smile...and she did. She didn't realize the expression had made its way to her face until Cavanaugh reciprocated with a smile of his own. This all felt so familiar, but Sarah cared less about why it felt the way it did and more about how to prolong it.

Prolong...long...ride...bus...Sarah's thoughts were singular, spaced out, but one thought came out through her mouth.

"Shit!" she exclaimed.

"What?" Cavanaugh grinned.

"My bus! What time is it?" she asked, frantic. Moments ago there'd been no thoughts in her head other than the stranger's name.

"Eleven o' five."

"What! It can't be...your watch must be fast! There's no way we've been standing here that long."

Sarah all but yelled at him now. Unbeknownst

to her, she'd been right about his watch. Cavanaugh, chronically late for everything, always set his watch fifteen minutes fast. However, the fact remained that her bus had left five minutes ago.

Sarah bolted in the direction of where her bus should have been. Her overstuffed backpack jostled from side to side, causing her to look a little unstable as she ran. Too panicked to worry about how she looked or falling on her face, she kept stride. The small station seemed to stretch longer as she ran, feeling like forever before she reached the door to the outside. Cavanaugh had taken off behind her, chasing her through the bus station. His long, casual strides were almost relaxed compared to her childlike running. Before she made it to the door, she could see out the window that her bus which had boasted a huge illuminated sign stating its destination had been replaced with another. Ignoring the evidence in front of her, she burst through the doors anyway. Winded and teary-eyed, she stood there, a helpless look smeared on her face as her shoulders slumped forward, and her chest caved in defeat.

Cavanaugh felt an ache for her, not because he couldn't help, but because of the pain drawn over her features. He also felt opportunistic at the chance to act on what he'd felt since...well, five minutes ago. He wanted a shot at taking care of the one individual, other than his horses, he'd ever felt compelled to provide for, keep safe, love. He felt the hot acids in his stomach churn and ascend at the word love for the second time since seeing her which was more than he'd ever experienced, let alone in one day... hell, one hour!

"Sarah?" he called, his voice almost timid. What in the hell was happening to him? He wasn't shy and he damn sure wasn't timid!

"What?" Her tone was harsh as she whipped her head around fast enough to make Cavanaugh dizzy. "This is your fault!" She pointed an angry finger at him. "If you had just let me kick that stupid machine, get my damned crackers, and get back on my bus, I'd be on my way to California right now! But, no, you had to come along with your southern charm and sexy smile, making me lose track of time. Now I'm stuck here in this nowhere town at this crappy bus station! Thanks a lot...Cavanaugh!"

Sarah reeled, spitting out his name like spoiled milk. All the while, adding a mock interpretation of his Texan accent fit for the insult she intended it to be. She had just admitted to him that she considered him charming and sexy, a fact he was, no doubt, aware of.

Cavanaugh smiled, following it with a laugh. He found her tirade both nubile and amusing. He had to concentrate not to allow his body to reveal his arousal.

He shifted uncomfortably, but it had nothing to do with the glare in her starburst eyes. He tried to assign them a color but couldn't. For a moment, Cavanaugh traced the contours of her oval-shaped face with his eyes. He watched as her anger spread from her neck to her face, coloring her ecru skin a shade of red.

Cavanaugh shifted again, trying to adjust himself so Sarah wouldn't notice the bulge in his pants. It seemed harder to do by the second, considering his thoughts. He deemed her stunning in the least conventional way—in a way that embodied all of her: her temperament, foul mouth, attitude, her sporadic reticence, the undeniable spark in her eyes and current pout at the lips, the way she teetered on the side of her foot like a nervous teenager. Cavanaugh could continue to make this list in his head and wondered how long it could be, yet he feared the answer. He opted to speak aloud before he lost her, something else that caused him a bit of anxiety.

"What in the hell is so funny?" she asked before he could say anything.

How did she manage to be so sexy? His mind had gone in another direction yet again. He kept thinking of all the things he wanted to do with her, to her. Parts of him wanted to rip off that backpack and throw it to the ground just so he could embrace her. Other parts of him wanted to tear off her clothes and throw her to the ground so he could penetrate her. With these two pieces of him warring with each other, other parts still wanted and yearned to do other things.

"If you would calm down for a minute, I can tell you," he managed to say, forcing the war within him to quiet long enough to speak over the words in his head and the words coming out of her mouth.

He paused, a craving for her rising within him. He wanted to take her into his arms and quell her rambling, angered mouth with a kiss that would awaken every part of her. The rest of him, the parts he could not identify, longed to take her heart into his soul, swaddle it, and make her love him.

She waited, still glaring at him, though softer. She teetered on the outside edge of her left foot, having switched from the right. He almost gave in to the desire to kiss her, but he couldn't risk the scene. If she rejected him, that would make matters worse. The scene would, for sure, make its way back to his parents, and he was already on thin ice with them.

"I own this place," he said, at last. "I can arrange for you to get to...California, was it?"

Cavanaugh couldn't help the little smile that pulled at his lips. Although, something inside tugged at his spirit. Something that wanted to ask her not to leave. Something that wanted her to stay...with him, crazy as that seemed.

"Free of charge, of course."

"Yeah, right!" Sarah gave a mirthless laugh. "You own this building or the buses?"

"I am part owner of Greyhound and full owner of this crappy bus station, in this nowhere town, that I was born in." Cavanaugh's tone mocked her this time.

"Really?" Sarah challenged, incredulous, keeping her face passive—or so she thought.

Her mind moved faster than she could catch and hold on to one thought. What were the chances of her meeting the owner of Greyhound? Things like that didn't happen to Sarah. At least not to Sarah Elaine Evans.

"I only come to this location about once a month to check on things: repairs, scheduling, improvements, and such."

"You can start with that vending machine," she blurted out the snide suggestion.

Grateful when he laughed, she hadn't intended to offend him, not any more than she already had anyway. She'd insulted his station and his town, not to mention him. As headstrong as she could be on any given day, something about this man made her feel like she didn't have to be in charge. She felt she could relax for a change and let a man be a man. No doubt she needed practice. She'd been in the caretaker role for so long she couldn't see any other way of living her life or living life at all.

Cavanaugh Jones, she thought again. She wanted to give him a chance to take care of her, if for no other reason than to see how it felt. *I'd bet he'd be good at it.* That thought swirled around her head in an intoxicating way. Though she wasn't much of a drinker, she knew what it felt like to be drunk, and this felt quite close.

Cavanaugh had moved very close to her. So close, in fact, she could smell his breath. It smelled of citrus, like the peel of a lemon. As close as they were, she wanted to be closer. She wanted to know him the way no one else did.

Cavanaugh still held his grin in place when he spoke again, pulling Sarah from her thoughts:

"Fine, I'll start with the vending machine, just for you." He winked at her, sending a wave of chills over her body.

Sarah never did take that bus to California.

CHAPTER THREE

Sarah turned onto interstate ten, heading west. She drove the familiar route to the place she called home. The place she'd lived since the first day she'd met Cavanaugh. Sarah pulled the car around the side instead of the parking in front of the house. She didn't want to disturb Cavanaugh's parents, though his mother, Cynthia, rose with the sun to tend to their horses.

"Cav." Sarah nudged his shoulder. During the ride, he'd shifted from drooling on the console to slobbering on the window. "Cavanaugh," she called louder.

"Yeah!"

Cavanaugh snapped up his head, a line of saliva roped from his mouth to the steamy, wet window. He dragged his large palm across his mouth and cheek and then wiped the wetness onto his jeans.

"We're home. Get up."

"I'm up, I'm up."

Sarah walked around to his side of the car and reached for the door handle, but Cavanaugh opened it before she did, hitting her with the door.

"Ow!" Sarah grabbed her hip and let out an irritated sigh.

"What happened, love?"

"You hit me with the door." Sarah spoke through her teeth.

"I'm sorry, babe."

In one movement, Cavanaugh made it to his feet and shut the car door. The nap had bestowed a veil of sobriety upon him, at least enough to be concerned and maybe a little of something else.

"Come here."

Still standing with a hurt expression on her face, Sarah began playing his game. She became the hurt little girl, and he would make it all better. In so many ways, it proved true. It seemed whenever he came around, her hurt subsided like magic. Cavanaugh had a way of making her pain disappear, except of course, when he'd inflicted it. Those times were, for the most part, accidental and happened when he'd been drinking which he did often.

Cavanaugh eyed at Sarah from under his eyelids, beckoning her with lustful looks. She found him almost impossible to resist. She took one small, shy step forward as she held a steady, sheepish gaze; a look she knew he found enticing. A smile teased her thin, pale pink lips. A seductive smile she may have been unaware of, but it wasn't lost upon Cavanaugh.

"Come here, my little love bug," he coaxed, pulling her into him.

She went willingly into his arms. This game they played, if anyone were watching, looked true to form. His massive size in comparison to hers made them look like adult and child. Sarah's twenty-six year old body still looked much like that of a budding teenager.

Cavanaugh ran his hands down her back and took hold of her bottom with both hands. She giggled and burrowed into him. She could smell the faint residue of cologne, but for the most part she smelled the Maker's Mark Bourbon he favored and had been drinking all night. The moon, full and bright, lit the sky, shining on them like the spotlight of a theater stage.

Cavanaugh's desire grew with the passing seconds. Sarah could feel his manhood growing against her belly. She slid her hands under his shirt, eager to feel the heat of his skin on her fingertips. Cavanaugh made a low growl deep in his throat. He then spread his hands wide along her rear, placing his thumbs on her hips and lifting her from the ground, bringing them pelvis to pelvis. The kissing that began as a teasing calm became erratic and uncontrolled. Sarah wrapped her legs around Cavanaugh's waist, crossing her high-heeled feet at the ankles. Cavanaugh circled one arm around her torso while the other moved along her bottom. All the while, his excitement continued to grow, pressing into the softness below Sarah's waistline.

Unwilling to take one hand off Sarah, Cavanaugh kicked the car door shut with his foot and walked them to the door of their three-bedroom apartment that doubled as the pool-house, although they almost never used it as such.

The door to their apartment—most often unlocked—just took a swift turn of the wrist for Cavanaugh to open it. The door swung open and slammed into the wall behind it with a loud bang. They both snickered as Sarah kicked it closed with her foot. Amid ravenous kisses, she removed the blazer Cavanaugh always wore. Sarah often thought of him as a character from the cartoons, having a closet filled with the duplicates of the same outfit. Yet, every day, he threw open the closet doors and pondered over what to wear. That would be her Cav. He had a blazer for every pair of pants and jeans he owned, and in every color imaginable. He wore them to work, to church, to the bar, and sometimes to bed, with the exception of nights like these.

As his blazer fell to the floor, Sarah fiddled with the

buttons on his shirt while kicking off her heels at the same time. Cavanaugh's hands had made their way inside her shorts without undoing a button or zipper. He massaged her buttocks and pressed her against his fly. She groaned. When he, at last, set her down on her bare feet he wasted no time undoing her buttons. Instead, he just yanked her shirt over her head and let it fall from his fingers.

A pleasured sigh escaped him and, for a moment, the upper half of his body went somewhat listless. He admired her bare breasts, gazing at them as though he hadn't seen them before.

"God, I love you," he said, his voice husky with desire.

His profession of love wasn't all love, although he did mean it. Lust and the fact that she hadn't worn a bra also fueled his words, lessening his task of getting her naked.

"Not as much as I love you."

"Wanna bet?" Cavanaugh laughed, as did Sarah, and they were skin to skin in less than a minute.

Both were passionate lovers; however, each seemed to be the conduit of heightened intensity to the other. They were a fierce mixture of extremes, which made for an explosive pair, in and out of the bedroom. In addition, neither of them were quiet lovers. Their living quarters were separate from the rest of the estate and Sarah couldn't have been more grateful for that.

Although, Sarah hadn't been a virgin when she'd met Cavanaugh, she still had a lot less experience than he did. Her list of lovers included two; she didn't care to know how long of a list he had. She found herself wondering about his sexual satisfaction at times. She could deem her pondering a waste of energy, because he never complained. In fact, he complimented her on a near constant basis. Not just in bed, but every day. He'd call her beautiful first thing in the morning, before she'd had a chance to brush her teeth.

Sometimes his accolades made her self-conscious. She wondered what he saw that she didn't, though she wasn't certain she wanted to know. In truth, Sarah hoped that his vision of her never changed, unless of course it changed for the better, something she couldn't see happening. Then again, she had never seen him coming either, and she could not be happier that he did.

As Cavanaugh planted a trail of kisses down Sarah's sternum, he took his time grazing her creamy, unmarred skin with his lips. Her flesh quivered under the tickle of his five o'clock shadow, which had evolved into a six-thirty shadow from so many missed days of shaving. Sarah liked it when Cavanaugh let his beard grow wayward and scruffy. Her hands and fingers often found a playground there.

As he continued his trek along her peaks and valleys, he reveled in the splendor she didn't see. He knew this because he always watched her dress. She had a grace about her movements, and her hidden insecurities revealed themselves in infinitesimal portions: a few extra strokes of her brush when her hair already looked perfect; the near unnoticeable adjustment of her clothes when they were positioned in all the right places; how she closed her eyes in the mirror for a long moment just to open them again and look at herself, he presumed, with a fresh set of eyes. Oh, how he wished she could use his. Then she'd know. She'd know the treasure she is and would never again second-guess herself...not for a moment.

After a long and loud sexual "session"—as they sometimes called it—the two of them collapsed into heaps on the floor. They had made it to the bed and off again along with the blankets and pillows that made it up—all but one. Their limbs overlapped and twined together like a hand-woven basket. Sarah found the softness of Cavanaugh's chest and lay there. It didn't feel as uncomfortable as it looked, nor did it feel hard and chiseled as she'd thought when she first met him that day in the bus station. She drifted to sleep as she thought about that day, the beginning of her eternal date with Cavanaugh. Had she, indeed, been swept off her feet like a character in some distorted, dysfunctional Cinderella story?

"Can I take you to lunch?" Cavanaugh asked.

"Yes, you can take me to lunch. Lunch in California."

Sarah still spat words at him, angry and frustrated.

"Fair enough." He nodded with a smile. "But considering it's such a long way, I think you'll be pretty close to starved before we get there." As if someone had just cued the sound effects, Sarah's stomach grumbled. "At least part of you agrees with me."

She stood quiet, unable to deny what her body had made known to the stranger, grateful that the other parts of her were quiet and hidden from him. She stalked past him towards the front doors.

"You'd better not take me anywhere to get crackers either!" she yelled behind her.

"My car's in the back." Cavanaugh pointed to a set of doors at the opposite end of the station.

He couldn't wipe the silly grin from his face. He found this woman so amusing and arousing, her anger enhancing what he felt. Sarah whirled around and stomped back towards him, making a point to bump him with her backpack.

"No crackers, I promise," he said as he stumbled back on his heel.

Cavanaugh took her to a late lunch at a place called Boudros, in San Antonio, four hours from where they started in Abilene. Sarah, stunned into silence upon entering the eatery, stood at the threshold with wide eyes. She'd never seen such a beautiful restaurant. Of course, her travels had taken her no farther than Charleston, South Carolina and as far as she knew, no place like Boudros existed there.

Colored tea light lanterns sat at the center of almost every table in the restaurant. Others held short vases with exotic flowers growing out of them. The hostess guided them to a room exploding with color. The patterned wallpaper displayed odd shapes that Sarah couldn't name. Lamps hung over the tables in various prints, fabrics, and metals. The chandeliers also boasted striking colors.

As beautiful as Sarah thought it to be, she couldn't stifle her desire to sit outside on the waterfront. Tables set up along the water's edge were shaded by oddly shaped umbrellas. Sarah's smile widened as the hostess redirected them to the outside tables at Cavanaugh's request. How did he know? Sarah thought as she all but bounced to their seats. She watched the ducks float on the surface of the water for a long moment before turning her attention to Cavanaugh.

"This is one of my favorite restaurants." Cavanaugh gazed at the river.

"I can see why." Sarah smiled.

"So, California, huh? That's a long way from South Carolina, don't you think?"

"That's exactly the point. I wanted to get as far from Beaufort as possible. I need a big change and the only way I could see a big change was to move to a big city."

"San Antonio's a big city..." Cavanaugh spoke in a low tone, almost as if he hadn't intended for Sarah to hear him.

She almost asked him what he'd said, but decided to take a moment to decipher his quiet words. She wondered what he meant by that statement, if anything at all. Both Cavanaugh and Sarah went silent, staring at the ducks again.

While Sarah continued to wonder, Cavanaugh contemplated the possibility of Sarah staying in San Antonio. Where would she live? What would she do? How would she feel if he asked her to stay? How would he feel? At the moment, he felt confused by his emotions and more by the fact that he had any for this woman. He'd never been so rash, at least not in this way. Before he could put a cap on anything he felt, he blurted out:

"Why don't you just stay here?"

"What?" Sarah gave an incredulous laugh. "That's crazy!"

"Not any crazier than uprooting and moving to California on a Monday."

Sarah couldn't argue that point. She had packed up all she could carry and boarded a bus headed across the country without telling her father. It was the craziest thing she'd done to date. However, instead of resisting the implication of Cavanaugh's suggestion she countered:

"Yeah, but...where would I live? And work? I don't know anyone here. I don't know anything about San Antonio and I—"

"You can live with me."

Words kept falling out of Cavanaugh's mouth, much to his own disbelief. He couldn't seem to control his tongue, or his emotions.

"You don't have to worry about work if you don't want to."

Sarah stared at him with her mouth agape and her brows scrunched together. An expression of pure astonishment coated her face. In a twist of irony, Cavanaugh's face looked just as staggered as hers, if not more.

As they sat frozen in place, the waiter brought out

hot plates of food, setting one in front of each of them. Sarah knew she hadn't ordered anything, and she didn't remember seeing Cavanaugh order anything either. Of course, too stunned to speak, she remained quiet, looking at the food with glazed eyes.

"You're kidding, right?" she asked after another long moment.

"It's just seafood," Cavanaugh spoke with an air of nonchalance. "It's what I usually order. I come here all the time. Unless I tell someone otherwise, they bring my usual. Try it."

Cavanaugh gestured to the steaming plate in front of Sarah, urging her to taste the dish. He'd already picked up his fork, poised to dig in.

"Not that! I'm talking about staying here...with you."

A tinge of excitement burst within him at the sound of her saying his words aloud. As though she'd given him the answer he wanted. The thought made him anxious, made his blood pump a bit more fiercely through his veins.

"You can't be serious. You don't even know me. I could be..." Sarah struggled to come up with a believable alter ego. She looked around as though looking for someone to fill in the blank for her, circling her hand in the air.

"A murderer?" Cavanaugh suggested, humor

lighting his eyes.

"You don't know! Maybe. Or I could just be a little, or a lot, crazy." Sarah paused, looking at her food for the first time. She picked up her fork and shuffled some of the items around. "You're not very funny, you know."

"I'm not trying to be funny."

Cavanaugh spoke in a calm tone, his words falling into his plate while he stared, as though he could see them settling onto his food like flakes of pepper. Afraid he'd lose his nerve if he looked up but more afraid he'd say something crazier, although he couldn't imagine anything farther fetched than this.

"I mean it, Sarah," He paused, savoring the taste of her name on his tongue. "Stay here...with me. Let someone take care of you for a change. Let me take care of you."

So much for putting a lasso on the crazy.

Cavanaugh's last statement held the most appeal to Sarah. She'd disclosed most of her boring life's story to him on the ride from Abilene. Telling him about her vacant mother, her father whom she'd left behind and her not-so-wild stories of growing up in South Carolina.

She continued to stare at him. Part of her didn't believe the words coming out of his mouth and other insane parts of her couldn't believe she'd considered the ridiculous idea. Despite all the crazy, half-baked, irrational thoughts, Sarah responded to Cavanaugh's offer.

"Okay."

She managed to get the single word out of her mouth and couldn't believe she'd said it.

"Really?" Cavanaugh couldn't believe it either. "You'll stay?"

Sarah didn't trust herself to repeat the word aloud, so she opted to nod her head "yes" instead. Afterwards, she put a forkful of food into her mouth to keep from saying anything else. Who knew what else she'd agree to at this rate. The scenario had already moved beyond ridiculous, not to mention impractical, but she still wanted it. She wanted it more than she wanted California.

CHAPTER FOUR

As Cavanaugh sprinted across the lawn, he tried to train his mind on finding Sarah instead of thinking on what might have happened to her. He redirected his thoughts away from those which included the possibility of her being hurt or bleeding or worse. He thought of her sprite-like image, laughing like a child at his feeble jokes. He thought of her love of puzzles. Oh, how she loves puzzles...any kind of puzzle: crossword, word search, jigsaw, you name it. Sarah also harbored a fondness for horses. He remembered how her eyes lit up the first time he'd taken her to the stables. Sarah's love for horses stemmed from one of her happiest childhood memories. She'd told Cavanaugh the story several times.

Sarah's eighth birthday fell on a warm day in spring.

Her father, Gray, had planned a grand surprise for which he'd arranged more than a month in advance. The torture of secrecy weighed on them both. Gray couldn't hold a secret if it had a handle on it and you gave him a pair of vice grip pliers. Sarah, on the other hand, always knew when Gray hid something from her. Anytime Sarah suspected Gray of 'holding out', she'd prod in that incessant way she always did, causing Gray to struggle more in keeping his lips sealed. This time around, he'd told little white lies to mask the real surprise. He'd given Sarah tiny clues, which didn't reveal much and danced around the 'real' plan.

Sarah and her father shared a trailer on a little piece of land, near the military base where Gray had once lived. As a young man, Gray lived in the barracks until he'd married Elaine. He'd bought the land with the intent of building a house for his family—until Elaine walked out, taking his motivation with her. Elaine left behind disintegrated dreams, a young girl, and much heartbreak.

Gray decided to buy a trailer in lieu of building a house with rooms he'd never fill with anything but his vacant heart cries. He didn't need that much space to move about and think of all the things he no longer had. Of course, he had his darling girl, Sarah, and he did the best he could by her. Living in the trailer kept him close to her, and he'd sit down with her and make plans to take road trips for holidays and during the summer. Alas, they never did.

On the morning of her birthday, Sarah sat up in bed as though she'd been caffeinated. With a quick brush of her teeth, she ran towards the front door, trailing a wave of rushed encouragements at Gray as she ran by.

"Daddy, Daddy! Let's go! C'mon!" She dragged out the last word in her best whiny voice. "Dad!"

Gray hadn't opened his eyes, let alone gotten dressed. Sarah, on the other hand, dressed the night before, sleeping in her clothes to save time. Now, she bounded to the car with unrestrained joy and anticipation. Though she hadn't known what to expect, she knew it had to be good because her father had managed not to tell her. Any other time he would have spoiled whatever surprise he had by blurting it out or giving in to her incessant inquiries.

When Sarah got home from school the day before, she'd made certain to tidy the trailer; afterwards she took her bath and picked out one of her favorite outfits. She felt so lucky that her birthday fell on a Saturday. That meant no school and no waiting for an appointed time to receive her gifts. She dressed in a pair of jeans and a dark purple shirt with colored flowers printed across the front. She put on her socks and almost put on her shoes too, but decided against it because of all the rainfall from the day before. Her muddy sneakers had hardened dirt packed into its ridges at the soles. Their trailer sat on a soft patch of earth, which always became sodden with the rains, no matter how heavy or light. It amazed Sarah that the ground had not yet swallowed them and their trailer or perhaps left it on a permanent tilt. Sarah liked the squishy sounds her shoes made in the mud, but not the mess it made in the trailer or of her shoes.

Bursting out the door, Sarah took a long leap over a particular sinkhole that she knew had filled with water. Without missing a step, she flung the car door open, climbed into the passenger seat and fumbled with the seat belt of their old, rusted 1972 Oldsmobile Cutlass Supreme. She sat there, and for the hundredth time tried to find the "supreme" qualities of the old car. The door panels along the edges were withering away with rust. Years of exposure to the elements had left the car's color almost indistinguishable. It looked like it used to be a periwinkle blue, or an indistinct shade of green or gray. Who knew? Old is all Sarah could see. She snickered sometimes when she thought of the make of the car and how accurate its name had become. At one time, they'd owned a newer car, but that left with Sarah's mother, never to return. She couldn't remember much about that car, except its color: red. Like the scarlet letter. Another accurate label for the car and its owner.

Honk! Honk! Sarah, fraught with impatience, lay on the horn, blaring its call and causing drivers passing by a bit of panic.

"Gal, if you don't calm down, we won't be going anywhere!" Gray yelled from the open door that Sarah hadn't bothered to shut.

"Yes, sir," she answered in defeat.

"Now, just give me a minute to get into my britches and we can leave." Gray disappeared inside, leaving the door ajar.

Sarah couldn't stand the thought of having waited so long to lose out on her surprise, so she sat on her hands and thought of the things it could be. Of course, she had no real clue. Her imagination went on a wild trek while her smile spread at the possibilities. Before long, Gray made his way outside and into the driver's seat of the car. Sarah bounced on the springy seats, still sitting on her hands, unaware of her actions.

"Hot damn girl, you got ants in your pants?" Gray asked.

"Just a few," Sarah eyes sparkled as she grinned. "Can we go now, Daddy?"

Gray laughed and started the engine. Although the body of their age-old vehicle was a sore sight for any eye, Arlene ran like a dream. Gray spent a lot of time under her hood making certain that all her parts were functioning as they should. Often, Sarah would stick her head under there too asking one question after another about how things worked.

"Whacha doin' now, Daddy? What does that do?

What's this called? And that? And what about that thing? Do you need the wrench? I know which one that is. Can you teach me how to...?"

Sarah's questions never seemed to stop and Gray never failed to answer. He liked that she had such a keen interest in cars, and since it looked like he'd never get that boy he'd dreamed about, Sarah would have to make due as his understudy. He'd told his friends on several occasions that he thought Sarah to be much better than some knuckle-headed little boy, having witnessed their male offspring with their rebellious ways. Not his Sarah. Not only was Sarah interested in cars, she cleaned too. She also tried to cook, although he wouldn't let her do too much. After all, she'd just turned eight.

Sarah spent the entire hour and a half ride bouncing in her seat. She never stopped moving, but she never asked anymore questions either. Her taut grin pulled her muscles so tight it made her cheeks ache. It matched the ache in her head from the rambling thoughts of endless gifting prospects. She rolled her window down to get some of the cool spring air on her flushed face. Gray told her she looked like a dog hanging out the window that way, her long, dark locks blowing in the wind. She may as well have had her tongue stuck out. Gray harbored an impatience that rivaled Sarah's. As her anxiety rose about discovering her surprise, his spiked as well in excitement to reveal it to her.

Gray showed visible relief when they crossed the county line into Charleston. A few miles beyond the county line, he turned onto a dirt road. Sarah, at last, stopped her anxiety-ridden movements. Her smile faded as the images she'd imagined swirled away, blending into the dust that rose all around them. She went still, apart from the jostling of the car on the rugged road. Her disappointment surfaced as they traveled the long road that seemed endless to Sarah. As the nothingness stretched on, so did her disillusionment. Gone were her visions of wide smiles, giddy laughter, and elated disbelief.

"Daddy?" she called, her voice somber and quiet.

She didn't have a question. She had nothing she wanted to ask, but her tone spoke to Gray. He squirmed in his seat a little, much like she'd done for their short road trip. He pressed his lips together as he looked at the sad expression on her face.

"Just a minute, pumpkin. You'll see," Gray managed to say, a sly smile spreading across his face.

Sarah slumped in her seat. We're not even going into the city. She thought. There couldn't be anything out here worth doing. What could he have planned fun that started with a dirt road? Sarah's eight-year-old imagination couldn't conjure any joyous thoughts in such surroundings, until...

Her eyes went wide with wonder. She followed the

figures as they made their way across a large field. Sarah's mouth went slack as her head fell in line with the image that filled her eyes. Mesmerized, she couldn't speak, she could only stare. Her eyes followed a shiny, black horse and its rider galloping across the grassy expanse. Their movements seemed one in the same, their rhythms exact, and their happiness evident. Sarah thought it to be the most beautiful thing she'd seen in real life, except for the ocean.

"Daddy?" Sarah felt for her father's hand, while her eyes remained trained on the majestic creatures.

"Yes, baby," Gray answered the question she couldn't find the words to ask. Sarah squealed and threw her arms around Gray's neck with reckless exuberance, causing him to veer off the beaten path a little. "Hold on, honey! I know you're excited, but at least let me put the car in park."

Sarah returned to her relentless bouncing. The spark reappeared in her eyes and color to her cheeks. Gray laughed as he gazed at his only daughter. The moment turned out better than he'd imagined. As a single father and perpetually ill, Gray had not had the means or the wherewithal to do the things he'd dreamed of doing for Sarah. He'd expressed a fear of her teenage years. Though they were afar off, she had no mother for guidance and he was clueless. For now, however, he focused on her adolescent dreams, fulfilling them as best he could.

Gray wasn't a prideful man. He'd ask for help when he needed it and had little or no problem doing so. He would also ask for directions if he felt he'd gotten lost. Everyone who knew Gray liked him. Apart from his drinking, almost no one had any negative words to say about him, in or out of his presence. He'd acquired many friends during his serving years and had called on one of them to aid in giving his baby girl a very happy birthday.

Jeffrey and his wife Alice Wahl owned a horse farm. Alice had been an equestrian most of her life. She'd trained well and, in turn, trained her horses well. She had also been a competitive show jumper once, and horses were all she knew and all she'd ever wanted. While Sergeant Major Jeffrey Wahl served as a Marine Corps Recruiter on Parris Island in South Carolina, Alice procured her dream of owning and breeding horses. The two had been married for almost thirty years, having married just after graduating high school. Jeffrey, days away from signing up with the United States Marine Corps, helped plan the small wedding which they had in his parents' backyard. Their honeymoon took place at the local Marriott hotel and continued into their lifetime of shared happiness. They spent the first few years of their marriage 'on the run' as Alice often described it. It began in South Carolina, and then on to the School of Infantry in California, first assignment in Washington, D.C., the second in North Carolina. The list goes on to include two deployments: one to Okinawa, Japan and another to Liberia.

Alice, unable to bear the idleness of waiting for her husband to return from his deployment or his tour of duty, continued to revel in the other love of her life— equestrianism. By the time the journey brought them full circle, Jeffrey had been stationed at the base on Parris Island where he and Gray met and became friends. The couple purchased the very house they lived in now with Alice's dream in mind and had lived there almost as long as they'd been married. None of the Wahl's three children had known any other residence until they were adults and moved out on their own.

The baby of the family, Emily, still lived in the house where she grew up. She was who Sarah ogled astride the beautiful horse. Her curly, golden locks bounced behind her in the swirling breeze. Sarah could see the smile on her face as she rode by. Both of them, Emily and the horse, had muscled legs and perfect posture.

Sarah had her door open before Gray had shifted the lever to park. She aimed to jump out of the car, but the seatbelt yanked her back with a steady pull across the chest.

"Daddy, let go!" she said with impatience, but then realized that it wasn't her father who had a hold on her after all. Gray laughed at her as she fought with the buckle and belt, unable to get the seat belt off fast enough.

"It's not funny!" Sarah grinned, snickering at herself.

"This must be Sarah," Alice said, coming out to greet them. She'd been standing in the window when they drove up. "Happy birthday."

Alice stooped down to talk to Sarah, smiling at the pretty little girl who couldn't seem to keep still.

"Thank you." Sarah tried her best to be polite. Yeah, yeah. Can I get to my present now? She dared not be that rude, but she could think whatever she wanted.

"Hi, Gray. How are you?" Alice gave Gray a warm hug.

"Oh, hangin' in there. Thank you so much for doing this, Alice. I—"

"It's nothing. I'm surprised you hadn't brought her here sooner." She looked at Sarah. "She reminds me of Emily."

Alice smiled. She had a smile that could subjugate the toughest male exterior and it often did. Alice had never been hard to look at. Despite her age, the beauty remained. She kept her once blond hair, now silver, cropped just below her earlobes. Her eyes and hair were an identical shade of gray and her face had weathered the years with grace. She had lines around her nose from a lifetime of crinkling it when she laughed and lips colored red from always biting them in concentration. Her body rivaled that of a twenty-something athlete with toned legs, strong arms, and an overall svelte figure.

Just as Sarah began to get annoyed with Gray and Alice's cordial but brief exchange, Emily and her horse appeared again, this time in a slow walk as she approached them. Sarah intended to tug on the tail of Gray's shirt, but her hand hung in the air as if someone had tied a string around her wrist. Her arm dangled as she stared.

"Hi, Mr. Evans!" Emily said, alighting from her horse. "Hi, Sarah!"

"Hi, Em. Looking good out there!" Gray responded.

Sarah wondered why everyone seemed to know her, but she wasn't familiar with any of them. Of course, she'd met Mr. Jeffrey before, but why hadn't she been a part of this world?

"Thanks! Bethany is my favorite horse. She makes me look good." Emily stroked the horse's mane as she spoke.

Sarah, still in awe, couldn't find any words to speak to the beautiful woman who had gotten off the attractive horse. She just stood there with her mouth hanging open as everyone else's words swirled around her ears, but never made their way in.

"Hey, Sarah. Wanna get outta here and go see some horses? Get away from the grownups?" Emily whispered the last question as she winked at Sarah.

Sarah bobbed her head up and down, still unable to find any words of her own. Emily took Sarah by the hand, flashed a knowing smile at her mother and Gray, and led Sarah toward the stalls. Sarah found herself in a world of happiness she'd never known possible. Emily allowed her to make friends with a small pony they called Bit-Bit and then, surpassing all the birthday dreams Sarah had for this day, she got a chance to ride him.

Sarah fell forever in love after that, bugging Gray non-stop to visit the Wahl farm. A time or two Emily came to pick Sarah up and spent the day there, grooming and caring for the horses. Of course, she got to ride too, but after a time, it all faded into nonexistence. Once every so often, turned into once a year, and that turned into never again. It wasn't until Cavanaugh brought her home that she'd been reminded of how much she loved and missed being around horses. She jumped at the chance to help Cynthia any way she could, as long as she got to be in the presence of the horses.

Cavanaugh often woke up alone, his hands searching for Sarah in the morning, or sometimes afternoon, sunlight. Amid his grogginess, he'd never panicked because she hadn't been where he remembered. He always knew where she'd disappeared to, so it wasn't unusual for him to find the other side of the bed empty. Except, this time he didn't just wake up alone; this time he'd awakened saturated in someone else's blood. This time he had reason to panic, reason to wonder where Sarah had gone. Even still, he thought the most logical place to look first would be the stables.

CHAPTER FIVE

"Where's Sarah? Have you seen her? Did she go riding this morning?" Cavanaugh threw questions at the stable hand, his words coming out in a rush.

"No, Mr. Jones. I can't say that I have," the man answered, looking confused.

"Are any of the horses missing?"

"No, but I did find Casey muddy and roaming this morning. I just figured someone hadn't tied 'em up good. Miss Sarah does favor him. Rides 'em all the time."

Cavanaugh muttered a string of curses as he thought of all the horrible things that could have or might have happened to Sarah. He'd never given any thought to losing her. He knew he wasn't the easiest person to love, but Sarah made it look easy. She made loving him look effortless, likewise when he drank too much and blacked out.

Cavanaugh did a quick sweep of the property, looking around for his mother. He spotted her free longeing a young horse in one of the three round training pens they had on the property. He started to yell to her, but thought better of it, his eyes following the animal who trotted along the perimeter of the pen. He didn't want to startle the horse, so he ran full speed toward the pen, startling her instead.

"CJ." Cynthia's eyes were wide when she turned to Cavanaugh who'd slowed his pace just enough to keep from slamming into the gate. "What is wrong with you? Why are you running around like a crazy person?" She reined in the horse, stroking him to keep him calm.

"I can't find Sa—" he began, but couldn't finish his sentence for trying to catch his breath. Cavanaugh put his hands on his knees and dropped his head as he huffed.

"Sarah...have you seen her?" He looked up. The words came out of his mouth on individual puffs of breath. "She...she...I have to find her. There was blood...and...she's gone. I can't—I can't—I need her." Cavanaugh had trouble making sense and it showed on Cynthia's face.

"What are you talking about, son? Why are you so upset? The girl is fine. She went for a ride this morning after we fed the boarders." Cynthia looked both confused and unconcerned.

"She's fine? You saw her?" Cavanaugh stopped breathing for moment.

"Yes, CJ, calm down. I know she's cute an' all, but I don't know what the big deal is. You can stand to be away from her for a few minutes, can't you?" Cynthia spoke in Texas drawl heavier than Cavanaugh's, but she often interchanged it for a more controlled tongue to save face in front of her colleagues and associates.

"Ma!" He let out the breath he'd been holding.

"What?" Cynthia shrugged her shoulders. "She's just a girl, I'm sure you can live without her for a day."

Cavanaugh couldn't stand the thought of not having Sarah, let alone trying to find someone like her. From the day he'd met her, he couldn't fathom having to let her go.

The day Cavanaugh met Sarah was a day he wouldn't soon forget, if ever. It would prove to be longest date he'd ever had. Any other time, any other day, hell, with any other woman, this would have sent Cavanaugh into tidal waves of absolute hysteria—be it terror or amusement.

He might have either hyperventilated or had uncontrollable fits of laughter at the thought of commitment, if not both. Sarah, however, had an unspoken hold over him that he seemed powerless to contest.

Seated at Boudros on the Riverwalk, Cavanaugh and Sarah occupied the table long enough for a shift change, talking about whatever came to mind. Cavanaugh couldn't remember having ever felt so comfortable or forthcoming with the opposite sex, not since his adolescent years. Cavanaugh bathed in her presence, soaking up the moments he had with her. He didn't want this beginning to end with absence or trips across the country for pilfered moments of face-to-face time. He felt dizzy, intoxicated. He'd become irreversibly sozzled on the moonshine named Sarah Evans.

When at last they vacated the table where they'd had lunch, Cavanaugh took Sarah for a walk along the river. He guided her by the waist as they strolled, his arm resting upon her frame. He felt content there; unhurried, unfazed by who might see them, lost in the best way. He'd intended to take her for dessert, but found himself headed towards the county offices. Sarah didn't ask any questions. She walked next to him, rambling on about her friends back home and sharing her teenaged memories. He stared at her, while yet another impulsive thought filled his head. The corner of his mouth turned up into a grin as he watched her speak, oblivious to what was coming next.

Truth be told, he'd been oblivious too until he came face to face with Neil Creatwood.

Neil and Cavanaugh had been roommates in college and now sparred on the county's local basketball team. They never played on the same team. Each of them loved and valued the rights to shit talking the loser. Aside from being Cavanaugh's friend, Neil also happened to be a San Antonio, Bexar County judge. Cavanaugh and Sarah strolled inside the county building and into Neil's office.

"Got a minute?" Cavanaugh asked Neil as he gave him a half hug, patting him on the back.

"Yeah." Neil gave a side glance to the woman standing next to Cavanaugh. His eyes roved over her before returning to his friend.

Cavanaugh turned to Sarah: "Give me a second, okay, Sarah?"

"Sure." She retreated to the adjacent room.

"Nice!" Neil nodded in approval as soon as the door shut behind her. "What's up, man! Ready for the game next Saturday? It's time to give up your rights."

Neil laughed, but stopped short when Cavanaugh didn't join in. He looked at the serious expression on his friend's face and replaced his smile with a look of concern.

"Is everything okay? You're not in any trouble are

you?"

"Not yet," Cavanaugh answered, looking somewhat amused.

"Aw, shit." Neil's tone sounded teasing, but everything else about him conveyed seriousness. "Do I need to sit down?"

"I want to get married," Cavanaugh blurted out, noting how different the words sounded when he said them aloud.

Cavanaugh thought he should feel something adverse, something opposing his confidence when he said those words, but he didn't. He waited a full minute before speaking again. Despite his confidence, he still needed a moment for the words to settle, not just in Neil's head, but his own. He never imagined himself saying those words, and now they were out there in the universe. Maybe not so much the universe as Neil's office, but out there nonetheless. The most amazing part wasn't the words themselves but that Cavanaugh had meant them.

"I'm sorry, you want to do what?" Neil's tone rang incredulous. "I thought you said the 'm' word."

A taunting flicker lit Neil's eyes as he waited for his friend to respond. Cavanaugh had pranked Neil before, it wouldn't have been the first time. Cavanaugh recognized the familiar look, knowing Neil expected him to burst into laughter at any moment but he didn't waiver. He stood firm in front of Neil without a smile or spark of humor anywhere. Neil's emerging smile shifted to a crooked grin, but then faded altogether.

"What, you're serious?"

"I think so—"

"What do you mean, you think so? You don't think so when you're talking marriage!"

"Her name is Sarah." Cavanaugh ignored Neil's outburst. "I can't let her leave. I can't let her go to California. That's just too far away...from me. I want her here more than I've ever wanted anyone or any one thing."

"Is that her?" Neil lowered his voice to a whisper as he pointed at the closed door where Sarah waited on the other side. Cavanaugh nodded. "How long have you known this girl? What the hell did she do to you? She must have some good—"

Cavanaugh put up his hand to stop the ascent of assumptions and insults on their way out of Neil's mouth. A warning flickered in his eyes as he looked at the judge. Silence built a wall between them as each sized up the other. Neil lifted his hands in surrender. It appeared that this was the one woman he hadn't the freedom to speak ill of and someone Cavanaugh seemed quite serious about. Serious enough to marry.

"Can you do it? Now?"

"Have you gotten the paperwork done yet?" Neil asked.

Cavanaugh felt certain Neil already knew the answer to that question, but asked as a way of trying to dissuade him from such an irrational act.

"No."

"Man, that's your first order of business. You know I—"

"Come on Neil. I know you can bend the rules. I've watched you do it." Cavanaugh pled with Neil, cutting off his objections. Although he hated the thought of begging, he kept talking anyway. "We'll come back first thing tomorrow morning and fill out all the papers you can shove at us. Just do this for me. Please."

"If that's the case, why don't you just wait until then? I'll be here bright and early."

Peering at Cavanaugh, Neil waited but Cavanaugh had made up his mind. In a battle of wills against him, Neil would lose. No one had more of an iron will than Cavanaugh.

Cavanaugh stared at Neil, a determined look carved onto his face and into his stance. He watched as the judge gave away his telltale signs of surrender. On the bench,

Neil hid these signs well, but with friends, he lived a more transparent existence. It began with him gnawing on the inside of his right cheek, and then his eyes shifted back and forth from one object, to the target, and back again. The final signs of victory: a long exhaled sigh and ruffling of his thinning blond hair.

"Yes! I knew I could count on you!" Cavanaugh cupped Neil's face in his hands and kissed him full on the mouth.

"Ugh! You disgusting bastard!" Neil swiped at his mouth with the sleeve of his shirt until his lips and the surrounding area became inflamed.

"Oh, and one other thing...you can't tell my parents. Or anyone else for that matter."

"You know Cynthia is going to have your hide for this."

"I know. She'll probably scalp us both and then have us stuffed and mounted." Cavanaugh chuckled as he turned on his heel to exit. "Now, I just have to ask the bride."

"You haven't asked her yet!"

"Nope! But I'm sure she'll say yes. Now go on and get yourself ready. You have a wedding to perform!"

Cavanaugh left Neil standing there looking aghast,

astonished as he exited the room. He opened the doors to see Sarah pacing the tile floor. She looked nervous. Shouldn't he be the one nervous?

"Do you have a dress in that bag?" Cavanaugh's eyes darted to the over-sized sack she insisted on carrying with her.

"Yeah." Sarah looked down at her bag.

Taylor-Lynn's grandmother had always told the girls to never travel anywhere without keeping a clean pair of underwear and a change of clothes with you at all times, and a toothbrush.

"If you have to stuff a dress into your handbag, that works too," she'd said. "That way you're never left assed-out if something happens."

Sarah giggled aloud. Having followed the woman's advice she had, indeed, crammed a sundress into her carrying bag along with a pair of shoes and, of course, a travel-sized toothbrush kit.

"Why?" Sarah had a perplexed look on her face.

"Can you go and put it on for me?"

"Are we going somewhere else?"

Sarah eyed him, replacing her perplexed expression with one of suspicion. Cavanaugh noticed the change, certain she wanted to ask why he'd asked her to change, why he'd brought her to the county office. All questions he didn't want to answer. He hoped she wouldn't ask and just play along, that she would just think they'd come to pay his friend a quick visit or that he'd made plans for them to go to dinner, though they'd just had lunch. He decided not to give her the chance to speak up.

"It's a surprise," Cavanaugh said, in an effort to keep from telling her what he had cooked up, because he definitely hadn't planned it. "Can you just change for me, please?"

"All right." After a long pause Sarah answered Cavanaugh. His imploring eyes seemed to ease her into compliance. "Where can I change?"

Cavanaugh pointed down the hall, ignoring the skepticism in Sarah's tone. What he didn't know was that Sarah loved a good surprise. It had been a long time since someone had surprised her. A sly grin inched its way across his face as he watched Sarah saunter to the bathroom, located at the end of the long corridor.

"Just wait for me right out here when you're done, okay?" Cavanaugh yelled to her.

She turned and gave a simple nod of her head. At that, Cavanaugh took off down the stairs and out the front doors. He made it across the street in less than a minute, frantic in his search for a store where he could buy a ring or something like it. After poking his head into several shops and cursing about that section of the Riverwalk being void of any type of jewelry store, he ducked into a little shop that sold gypsy items like earth stones, crystals, and such. He scanned the displays and peeked into the glass boxes before he found a shimmering mood ring. He hated to get her such a cheap trinket, but he had to give her something. He promised himself that he'd buy her a real ring when he had sufficient time to shop for one, but for now, the mood ring would have to do. He bought a shimmery one for her and a plain one for himself. After all, you can't get married without rings, right? The cashier rang Cavanaugh up to a whopping $27.82 as he stood at the counter with beads of sweat dripping from his temple.

"Can I get you anything else?" she asked as she began to bag his items.

"No, just those."

He took the little plastic boxes from her hand before she could drop them into the bag, tossed two twenty dollar bills on the counter, and dashed out the door.

"Thank you, ma'am," he yelled over his shoulder.

Cavanaugh raced back across the street to the county building, taking the stairs, two, sometimes three at a time to the landing. Business hours were over and the building sat empty, leaving nothing to absorb the loud bang of the heavy doors as he bolted through them. He ran up one more small flight of stairs, and as he jumped up the final few, he tripped on the last stair and almost fell flat on his face. If he weren't so vain, there's a chance he would've ended up with a broken nose or bruised chin, but he'd managed to keep his face from smacking the hard floor.

Cavanaugh took that moment to pause and catch his breath just in time to lose it again. Sarah looked a vision in blue. When he looked up, he found her taking measured steps in his direction, freezing him there at the top of the stairs, conveniently on one knee. She wore a strapless, powder blue dress that stopped just above her knees in the front but the longer length in the back swept her ankles. The fabric clung to her body in enough places to outline a sultry silhouette. She'd also changed shoes and had donned a pair of nude colored high-heels. Cavanaugh wondered where she'd hidden those. Her hair, now pulled up off her neck, made her look more appealing than she had before.

"Wow," he said. "You look good enough to eat."

"Thank you. What are you doing on the floor?"

Sarah, by now, had made it to Cavanaugh, who still knelt where he'd fallen. He hadn't moved an inch, transfixed by Sarah's evolution. He dug in his pockets with clumsy fingers while stammering over incomplete words that never came together to form coherent ones.

"Are you okay?" Sarah scrunched her brows together as she looked at him. "You're sweating."

"Yeah. I—I'm fine. Better than fine, really. I haven't felt this good in a while." He managed to make some sense. "Uh, Sarah, I want to ask you somethin'..."

His drawl became heavy as he searched for the proper words to say. He'd never done anything like this before. Hell, he couldn't recall ever having told a woman he loved her...not in truth anyway.

"Okay, but do you have to do it from down there? Get up."

Sarah reached for him. As she did, her sack slid down her arm and to the floor next to him. He didn't move to get up. Instead he took her hand for a second, removing her arm from the loops of its handle. She gave him a strange look, a warranted expression because his behavior classified as a little weird.

"Well, uh, you see. Hmm, I don't really know how to say this or—I really don't know what I'm doin'. I'm just gonna come right out and say it."

Cavanaugh shook his head.

"Ahem," he paused. "Sarah?" he paused again. "What's your middle name?" He stopped his baffling conjuncture of words to ask.

"Elaine. What the hell—?"

"Sarah Elaine Evans...will you be my Mrs.? Marry

me, I mean." Cavanaugh had fumbled his words long enough to compile a few. Extending the ring to her, he waited for an answer.

Sarah belted out a loud laugh, filling the empty hall behind them with the joyous sound.

"This is a joke, right? Is that what you and your friend were talking about in there? You guys are pulling a prank on me?"

She forced the questions out through intermittent laughter. When she looked down at him, still on one knee, holding a ring in his shaking hand, her face went flat. She looked around, finding herself amused, but no one laughed with her. Sarah's humor faded. No one came bursting out of closed doors. No cameramen or microphones. No noise except that of her dying laughter. Cavanaugh still had not moved. He had been down there for a while, his knee pressed into the concrete.

"You're serious?" Sarah queried. "Really serious?"

"As a Texan is about barbecue."

"You want me to marry you?" Sarah, so dumbfounded, could think of nothing else to say apart from asking one question after another.

"That's what I'm askin'."

"You want to marry me?"

"Doesn't matter how many ways you phrase it darlin,' the question is still the same." Cavanaugh didn't trust that he wouldn't screw the whole thing up by asking the entire question again. "So, will ya?"

Sarah took another look at the ring between his giant fingers.

"I'll get you a real ring, baby, I promise. This is just for now, being such short notice and all."

"I—I, I've never been proposed to before. I— Cavanaugh, are you sure about this? I mean, we—I never thought anyone would..."

Sarah couldn't seem to collect her thoughts enough to make sense either. Her heart went aflutter, and her mind jumbled. Her emotions were like goulash, unable to decipher one bit from the next. She knew she wanted to be with him, as crazy as that sounded, and she'd already agreed to move in with him, hadn't she?

"I suppose this isn't any crazier than what we've already decided to do, huh?" Except that it was.

"Is that a yes?" Cavanaugh asked, aching for an answer.

"I suppose it is."

"So, you'll do it? You'll marry me? Right here, right now?" Cavanaugh took his turn asking question after question.

"What! Now?" Sarah didn't think she could be any more surprised.

"Yeah, Neil's in there waitin' on us. He's the officiant." Cavanaugh rose from his proposal position. "We're already here..." His light green eyes softened and he took both her hands in his. "And you did just say yes."

"That's why you wanted me to change?" Sarah looked down at her dress.

"Well, I wanted it to be special for you. I didn't want to ask ya while you were wearin' cutoffs and sneakers. You'd remember this and probably cuss me out later because you weren't dressed for the occasion."

Sarah didn't argue with that logic. In fact, she didn't say anything at all.

"Hey, Neil!" Cavanaugh yelled as he pulled Sarah by the hand and took her back to Neil's office. He opened the door and pulled her in.

"Well?" Neil asked.

"I told you she'd say yes!" Cavanaugh gloated.

"How did you know?" Sarah looked at him in disbelief.

Maybe he did know her; it certainly felt like it.

They had to have met in another lifetime because it all felt too easy. Cavanaugh gave her a wink of the eye, but never answered her question.

"Okay, well, let's get this show on the road," Neil said, his excitement apparent.

The couple walked hand in hand outside. Apart from a few seconds of Cavanaugh's chivalrous touch, it was the most contact the two had had since meeting that morning in Abilene. Now, hours later, 250 miles from where they began and more miles from where Sarah had intended to go, they walked outside of the Texas courthouse.

Just in front of the official building, a fountain spewed its waters up and over a three-tiered brim, where Neil had performed countless ceremonies. He'd brought the disposable camera he kept in his desk drawer that with him. As the sun set behind them, tinting the fountain waters orange, Neil pronounced them husband and wife.

CHAPTER SIX

Cavanaugh left his mother standing in the pen, dumbfounded. He didn't want to waste any more time asking questions about Sarah's whereabouts that no one had the answers to. Instead, he dashed back to the stables and hopped onto Thornton's bare back as if he'd stepped onto a spring board. He grabbed the horse's reins, gave him a kick and took off into the woods.

The Jones' mansion sat on more than twenty-five acres of land, housing two barns with thirty stalls between them. The Joneses both owned and boarded horses. The house contained five bedrooms with accompanying bathrooms. Its exterior, painted a stark white, looked bland, but the Spanish tiled roof gave the house a splash of color and character. The Guadalupe River ran along the eastern edge of the property, providing a constant, serene gurgle of water while creating a natural swimming hole in the warmer months of the year.

The apartment Cavanaugh and Sarah shared sat on its own, detached from the rest of the estate. The furnishings were modest, just like the furnishings in "big" house, consisting of carved wood and cowboy-esque furniture. Acres of land lay in bright green pastures, looking fit for a painting. Log fences surrounded areas where the horses grazed but the rest of the land poured into the woods adjacent to the property. A hard line of trees marked the dividing line, a line Cavanaugh headed straight for.

Once in the thicket, Cavanaugh began to yell for Sarah, slowing his pace as he looked for her. He made wide circles and then smaller ones, double and triple checking one area after another. He found nothing, heard nothing. He didn't want to lose hope, but he could feel it dwindling and he didn't know what else to do, where else to look. Where could she have gone? Cavanaugh began to think about all the blood he'd woken up in and how hurt she must be. According to the amount of blood, Sarah wouldn't survive if he didn't find her. Cavanaugh cursed to himself, frustrated and fearful. Thornton seemed to sense his mood and became anxious.

"Hold on, boy." Cavanaugh gave the horse a couple of pats on the neck.

After weaving through a few more trees, Cavanaugh decided to canvas the area on foot. He dismounted the horse and tied him to a nearby tree. While he searched, he became more distressed, fearing that he may have missed her.

"Sarah!" He called for her over and over again.

He received no answer. He all but tip-toed around, the forest floor crunching beneath his feet, listening for her answer. Cavanaugh looked around the woods, pausing at patches of leaves, pine straw, nests, anything that could potentially hide her. After a while, he went to a common trail, a trail the horses knew from memory. Walking the worn path himself, he continued to search for her in the surroundings in case she'd been thrown; of course, that wouldn't explain why she'd been bleeding before she left the house. None of it made sense.

Cavanaugh walked forward in a fog of formidable scenarios. One thought pushed aside for the other, fighting for the spotlight in his imagination, until he heard a faint noise. His ears perked and he whipped his head around, unsure if he'd heard something or if he'd conjured it up. He stopped walking and stood still, holding his breath to get a good listen. For as long as he could stand it, he didn't breathe. When, at last, he released the trapped air, he did so with a quiet whoosh, took another gulp of air and held his breath again. Cavanaugh closed his eyes and listened, forcing his other senses to sharpen.

A light breeze stroked his cheek as it blew by, making a soft rustle in the leaves of the trees. He noticed the aroma of oak wood in the air from the large Bur's that populated a lot of the land. There it was again! The same sound as before. His eyes flew open and he looked from left to right, knowing he'd heard something, although the sound had been as faint as a whisper. He recognized the noise, but wanted to ensure he hadn't imagined things, but that he'd heard the sound, heard Sarah.

"Sarah?" No answer. "Baby?"

He heard it again; a low clicking sound. A sound Sarah often made when she felt nervous or afraid. She would make a repetitious click in the back of her throat. The fact that it annoyed Cavanaugh so much made it easy to identify. Most of the time, Sarah seemed unconscious about the clicking, but it served as one of the ways Cavanaugh could gauge whether she felt apprehensive about something or at peace with it. The clicking noise continued, slow, faint, the time between each one stretching and constricting like a rubber band. He followed the sound, taking a few paces to the right and then straight ahead.

"Sarah? Is that you, love?" Cavanaugh asked, fearful that it would be her, but also fearful that it wouldn't be. He got an answer to his question when the clicking grew a little louder. "I'm coming, baby!"

Cavanaugh took off toward the sound, moving with renewed purpose. He tried to be quiet as not to drown out the sound but his efforts were in vain, thanks to the river. The closer he got, the harder it was to hear Sarah's subdued beacon. Afraid to make any more sound than necessary, Cavanaugh continued cursing to himself, keeping stride as he walked toward where he thought he'd heard the noise the loudest.

Standing a few feet from the river's edge, Cavanaugh couldn't hear anything but the rushing waters. Either the river washed out the noise or he'd made an error in thinking he'd heard it coming from that direction. Cavanaugh turned to make an about face, but stopped when he heard the sound again. He whipped around, but saw nothing. He made a series of measured turns while his eyes surveyed the area. Struggling to decipher the direction from which the noise had come, he paced a short distance and then another. He listened, wishing to hear the sound he'd once hated, while his eyes tracked across the leaf-littered floor.

That's when he saw it. In the brush, blending with the russet pine straw and dead leaves, Cavanaugh saw the tip of Sarah's riding boot. Its silvery tip reflected a beam of light, catching his eye. He took timid steps towards the boot and the closer he got, the more of Sarah he saw. Part of him had expected to find an empty boot, so the shock of finding her, seeing her, struck him in the chest like a spiked arrow. He thought he'd feel a sense of relief, but the horror built a fortress around that emotion. He stood for a long moment just staring at her body, heat burning the skin around his eyes, and for a moment, his vision blurred.

"Seej?" Cavanaugh found it difficult to speak, his voice coming out in a cracked whisper.

A garbled sound came from her tiny form propped up against a boulder. Cavanaugh stood at her feet, his eyes traveling over her as she turned her head toward his voice. The movement had been so minute that he would not have noticed it had he not been studying her.

"Baby?" He choked out, strangled by her appearance.

Sarah looked as if she had been beaten, her skin discolored and bruised. The large gash on her left temple could have resulted from a fall, but what about the rest of her? Sarah's right eye, swollen shut, bulged. The skin of her eyelid, tight with fluid, had darkened to a deep shade of purple, almost black. Cavanaugh's eyes roved over her as if she were a foreign entity from outer space. She lay there exposed, topless, save for her bra. Her shirt, saturated with blood, had been tied around her middle where she grasped her side. He looked at the slashes on her pants, which showed evidence of other cuts, soiling the fabric around them. Cavanaugh's eyes came to rest on her scraped and muddied boots, too stunned to move for a time, he just stared. He'd stood there so long that it caused a bit of numbness in his left leg where he'd been holding the brunt of his weight.

After another long minute, he found the courage to move. Squatting down next to her, he reached his arms out, only to draw them back. He couldn't decide how to touch her, where to touch her. When he reached out again, he positioned his arms opposite the way he'd attempted before, but drew them back once more. He considered Sarah for a few seconds and then grazed his finger at a point just behind her ear, a silent way of identifying himself. She made a low sigh, similar to the sound she always made when he touched her that way, one of their many unspoken languages.

"I'm gonna pick you up now, okay? I'll try not to hurt you," he said in a soft voice.

As careful as he could, Cavanaugh slipped his arms beneath her, having decided there was no pain-free way to touch her. He scooped Sarah up from the ground and into his arms. She groaned. Cavanaugh couldn't determine whether the groan meant pain or relief, but he apologized anyway.

"Baby, I'm so sorry."

With Sarah's battered, bleeding body against him, he found his way back to Thornton. Between steps, Cavanaugh examined his wife, noticing dark rings around her neck. He felt her blood spilling onto his fingers from the gash uncovered by the makeshift tourniquet. His fury and anguish grew with every new, morbid discovery. He hated the thought of having to get her onto the horse, but it was the fastest way back to the estate. Cavanaugh didn't know how long Sarah had been lying in the woods injured and feared it would be a waste of precious time trying to keep her in a state of relative "comfort," if that word could be applied. Sarah needed a hospital, hours ago.

"Seej. This is gonna hurt, okay?" he warned. "I'm sorry, but it's the quickest way back."

She remained quiet and unresponsive for a long moment. Then she breathed a heavy sigh and Cavanaugh knew she'd braced herself—as much as she could anyway. His stomach lurched as he prepared himself to move her, wishing for another way to transport her, but how could he? The thought of leaving her to get help made him feel just as sick as moving her onto the horse. He couldn't see any other way but to hoist her onto the horse in a somewhat prostrate position and he didn't trust that she could hold herself up for any length of time.

Cavanaugh raised Sarah up in the air as if sacrificing

her to the gods. His arms shook as he tried to keep his movements slow while holding her steady. He put her onto the horse, wincing as her pain became audible.

"Sorry, sorry, sorry, love."

Cavanaugh untied the horse, removed his shirt, and sprang onto the horse's back in one leap. Once there, he readjusted Sarah's body. Leaning her against his chest, he draped his shirt across her exposed torso and held her in place while he guided Thornton back through the woods toward his estate.

Cavanaugh whispered reassurances into Sarah's ears as they rode, a ride that seemed to take forever. He could not fathom what it must have felt like to her. He stole a glance at Sarah, doing a double take. It looked as if her skin had paled a few shades, maybe it had. He realized then that she hadn't made many moves or sounds for a while. His panic escalated, and he muttered a line of swears to himself wishing he'd thought to bring his cell phone. He could have called an ambulance and had it waiting or at least on its way by the time they got back to the stables.

"Henry! Henry!" Cavanaugh yelled at the stable hand as he burst through the brush and into the clear open field. "Follow me! Hurry up!"

Without hesitation, Henry mounted Casey and gave chase. His eyes rested on Sarah for a moment and his face crumpled. Cavanaugh didn't slow Thornton down until they were mere feet from the car with Henry right on his tail.

"Mr. Jones, what happened to Miss Sarah?" Henry jumped down from his horse and grabbed the reins of both his horse and Cavanaugh's. Although he hadn't gotten a good look at her, just a glance produced enough evidence to determine that Miss Sarah had been injured.

"I don't know, but I have to get her to the hospital, now!"

Henry put a supporting arm under Sarah as Cavanaugh slid down the side of the horse, making a soft landing on his feet.

"Holy shit!" Henry exclaimed in a low voice.

Cavanaugh kept his grip on Sarah as he looked from the car to the ground, wondering where the keys were. He peered into the window of the car and saw that Sarah's purse still sat on the floor, which meant the keys should be in there. Acting fast, Henry opened the passenger side door. Cavanaugh, handling Sarah like a precious, sleeping child he didn't want to wake, squatted down to put her into the car. He slid her listless body onto the leather, reclining the back. She still didn't make a sound, which worried Cavanaugh more than if she had. In the distance, Cavanaugh saw Cynthia approaching them, her gait casual and unhurried. He didn't have time to wait around just to give her an explanation, not that he had one.

"Tell Mother I'm taking her to the hospital," Cavanaugh instructed as he ran around to the driver's seat.

He couldn't get his knees under the steering wheel, evidence of Sarah being the last one to drive. For a quicker adjustment, Cavanaugh pressed one of the preset buttons on the door panel, grateful when the seat moved backwards on its track. He could never remember which setting belonged to him until his knees ended up in his neck. He knew Sarah had pilfered a setting for herself, but she'd never told him which belonged to whom, not that he'd remember anyway.

Cavanaugh liked that Sarah had claimed some of his things as her own and liked it more when she kept it secret. It felt like a joke within a joke to him. She thought he didn't know, but he was quite aware. He had also told her he didn't trust her driving his car, although he felt the exact opposite. He trusted her to drive it more than anyone, which is more than he could say for his parents, he didn't trust them to get behind the wheel as strange as that seemed. He'd told Sarah he didn't trust her to instill a little more caution to her driving. Truth be told, she drove better than Cavanaugh but he wasn't willing to admit that to her.

Closing his eyes, Cavanaugh pushed the button to start the car. He let out a heavy sigh when the engine purred to life and he thanked whatever higher power may have been keeping watch that he hadn't had to go searching for the keys. Before pulling off, he pushed yet another button, this one to open the heavy iron gates that led to their estate. He sped through the opening, almost knocking off his side-view mirror, as the gates had not fully opened yet. Cavanaugh had never been happier to have a sports car than at that moment, thankful he didn't have to waste time waiting for the transmission to catch up with his heavy foot.

He made it to the highway in what seemed like seconds, not realizing how fast he'd been driving until he just about missed the exit for the hospital. Glancing at the speedometer—which read 107 mph—he gave his blind spots a quick check and threw a protective arm around Sarah. Cavanaugh swerved across three lanes of highway as he aimed for the exit ramp, skimming by a slow-moving Hyundai in the process. Horns blared behind him and brakes squealed, but he ignored the surrounding sounds, disregarding the angry drivers as he blew through a couple of traffic lights. Within minutes, he pulled into the emergency lane of the hospital and jumped out of the car, leaving the driver's side door wide open. Yanking open the passenger door, Cavanaugh scooped Sarah into his arms again and ran inside, leaving the car running, doors opened and lane blocked.

"Sir, you're gonna have to move your car," a far off voice said.

"Not before you help my wife!" Cavanaugh's face

beamed red. "Can I get some help here? Why are you just standing there!" His desperation transformed his every word into a demanding roar.

"Okay, okay," someone said.

Cavanaugh had a hard time distinguishing which of the hospital personnel had spoken to him. Everyone sounded far away. He looked around, but no one seemed to be moving, at least not fast enough. Then he heard someone yelling instructions, but he didn't know whom they were for. Were they talking to him?

A bustling came close to him and he felt someone trying to take Sarah from his arms, but he couldn't focus his vision and refused to let her go. Voices sounded like the roar of a crowd, movement sounded like the crinkling of paper. He tightened his grip on Sarah, pulled her closer to him, feeling like she might slip away, out of his grasp or as though he'd drop her. Cavanaugh felt as if his brain were swelling. He could see nothing but red, feel nothing but panic. He needed to calm himself before he blacked out and he couldn't risk dropping Sarah or have the doctors bypass her to see about him. He had to make sure they helped her.

Someone tugged at Sarah again and the voices closed in on him.

"Sir? Sir? We're trying to get some help for your wife, but you have to let us. You have to let go. Sir, please."

The woman's voice pleaded with him. She spoke in a soothing tone, providing an anchor for Cavanaugh to hold on to for the moment. He could smell her light, powdery scent as it floated in the air around them. He shifted his eyes, struggling to bring her into focus.

"Sir, you need to let her go. These men are going to help your wife. What's her name?"

Cavanaugh squinted and then held his eyes wide, which helped to bring the nurse into focus. The milky brown fuzziness at the edges of her face transformed into sharp lines and prominent features. Her dark eyes were soft and her expression pleading as she touched his arms, tensed around Sarah's body. Cavanaugh's eyes floated down to where her hand rested on his arm and, as if jolted by electricity he realized why he'd come to the hospital. What he needed to do. His arms relaxed, but his expression remained fixed.

"What's your wife's name?" the nurse asked again.

By now, someone had removed Sarah from his grasp and transferred her to a gurney. Cavanaugh didn't see when it happened because he stood almost motionless, tethered to the nurse's voice.

"Sarah," Cavanaugh said, at last. "Her name is Sarah. Sarah Elaine. Sarah Elaine Evans...Jones. She's my... wife. She's my..." He choked on every other syllable.

"Okay, okay. Sarah Jones. So, you are Mr. Jones." The nurse kept a soft hand on him, guiding him into a chair. "Can you tell me what happened to Sarah?"

Cavanaugh wanted to respond, but he had no answer for what she'd asked, so he remained quiet. The woman took a seat next to him.

"Mr. Jones?" She peered around at him, trying to catch his gaze. "If I give you some papers, do you think you could fill them out for me?"

Cavanaugh nodded and answered, "Yes, I can do that."

The nurse didn't get up right away and in that moment, Cavanaugh's vision returned to normal. He took in his surroundings, including the soothing woman's name tag. It read Henrietta. A few seconds later, she stood and walked over to the nurses' station. She made her way back over to him in less than a minute and handed him a clipboard with a linked ball chain attaching a pen to it.

"Just fill these out as best you can. I'll be right over there if you need me." Henrietta pointed to the half-moon shaped desk where other nurses communed, sitting, chatting, and shuffling papers as if there were no emergencies.

With a pat on the shoulder Henrietta retreated, leaving Cavanaugh to his stack of forms. He gazed at the papers, holding the pen in his hand for a moment before filling the blanks in hurried scripts. He skipped the insurance portion of one form and then another. He'd never gotten around to getting any insurance for Sarah as he'd intended. He'd always just paid for whatever she needed when she needed it. Cavanaugh wouldn't think about the insurance except on the rare occasion when Sarah got sick but since she'd never had any serious illness, nor had she reminded him, it remained on their invisible 'to-do' list. Once he'd finished scribbling on the forms, he walked over to Henrietta and handed her the clipboard.

"How long do you think it'll be before I can see her?" he asked.

"I'm sorry, Mr. Jones, I don't know. They just brought her back there, so it may be a while. Let's give them a little time to work on her and I'll go check for you, okay?" They both nodded in agreement. "As soon as I know something, I'll tell you. Would you like me to get you some coffee or something else to drink while you wait?"

"No, no, that's okay. I'll get it myself. I need something to do anyway." Cavanaugh turned to walk away.

"Uh, Mr. Jones?" Henrietta called.

Cavanaugh turned on his heel. "Yeah."

"Would you mind moving your car for me? I think it's still running and that's the ambulance drop-off."

"Oh, shit! I'm sorry, I forgot all about that damned thing!"

"It's okay, happens all the time." Henrietta smiled.

As Cavanaugh moved his car to an official parking space, he thought of the horrid possibilities of what could have befallen Sarah while he lay unconscious in saturated sheets turned crimson. Who would have come in and hurt her? Who would want to? Did she scream? Did she call out for him? Why hadn't it woken him? Because he'd been drunk, as usual, that's why. Cavanaugh admonished himself for his drunken incompetence. For his imposed inability to provide one of his most important duties as her husband, protection. Right then, he made a vow to, at least, scale back his drinking. He wasn't naïve enough to try to convince himself that he would quit drinking altogether, in spite the grim situation.

Who could want to harm Sarah? Cavanaugh found himself asking the same question over and over again. Sarah, a mousy woman, remained quiet for the most part unless she felt angry or threatened. However, once she'd get comfortable with you then her mouth would run away with her. She wasn't crass or ill-tempered like Cavanaugh. If anything, it would be much easier to fathom someone trying to hurt him, but not Sarah. There's no telling how many disgruntled employees or ex-employees wanted to see him laid in a hospital bed. Sarah, just an innocent bystander, served as an enhancement to the happiness

Cavanaugh thought he knew. When she'd shown up, she'd endowed him with a new brand of happy.

The hospital's automatic doors opened with a whoosh as Cavanaugh walked back inside, pulling him from his rambling thoughts and redundant questions. He approached the nurses' station, searching for Henrietta. When he didn't see her he hoped she'd gone to get news about Sarah.

"Pardon me, ma'am? Do you mind if I use your phone for a quick sec? I'll just be a minute." Cavanaugh laced each word with his trademark charm and the nurse, who'd been staring at him, handed over the receiver with a bashful look and a bat of her eyelashes. "Much obliged."

He reached over the counter and punched in the phone number to his parents' house. No answer. He took it upon himself to choose a new line and dialed another number.

"Cynthia Jones." His mother answered on the second ring, her voice calm as if it were just an ordinary morning.

"Mother, it's me."

"CJ! What happened? Henry told me you were taking that girl to the hospital. Is she all right? Which hospital did you take her to?"

"We're at St. Luke's on Floyd."

"Why didn't you take her to—"

"Ma, really I'm not about to have this conversation with you."

"I'm just suggesting, son—"

"Ma! Look, I just wanted to call you and let you know where we were. Where's Dad? Does he know, did you tell him?"

"No, he's still in Brady. Left early this morning to pick up another boarder." Cynthia's tone oozed with nonchalance.

"You didn't call him?"

"What for?"

"What do you mean, what for!" Cavanaugh fumed. "You know, Ma, sometimes I wonder about you. I gotta go."

Cavanaugh hung up, banging the receiver into its cradle. She must have taken one too many Zoloft this morning, he thought. For the severity of the situation, Cynthia acted much too calm. Not five seconds after Cavanaugh hung up the phone, he saw Henrietta coming around the corner. Before he could utter a word, she motioned for him to follow her, taking him to the family waiting room. There, she gave him a very brief update on Sarah's condition.

"Your wife is in surgery," Henrietta began. "They have to repair the lacerations on her torso. There may be some damage to her liver, but the doctor will have to let you know for certain when he speaks with you afterwards." She paused for a beat, allowing Cavanaugh a few seconds to absorb the information. "That's all the news I have for now, but you can wait here and when the surgery is done the doctor will be able to explain the extent of her injuries to you more specifically."

"Well, how long is the surgery going to take?"

"I can't be sure, Mr. Jones, I'm sorry. I wish I had more to tell you."

"Me too." Cavanaugh sighed and ran his fingers through his uncombed hair. "Thanks for the update."

His statement of gratitude had been half-hearted, at best, if he'd meant it at all. The vague bit of information Henrietta gave hadn't answered any of his questions, nor had it appeased his worry. As the nurse exited the room, he plopped down into a chair and stared at the television mounted to the wall in the upper corner of the room. The images looked like colored blurs to Cavanaugh, moving this way and that, he couldn't focus on the screen. All he could see was Sarah.

He jumped out of the chair and paced the small room about twelve times before sitting back down. He switched chairs, paced some more, and then switched chairs, yet again. He seemed to be playing a game with himself, but he hadn't anything to do that would occupy his thoughts or his movements. In the middle of his fourth round of the self-imposed game, two uniformed police officers walked into the waiting room.

"Mr. Jones?" One of them asked. "Cavanaugh Jones?"

"Yeah?" Cavanaugh looked from one officer to the other, uncertain of whom had spoken.

"San Antonio Police Department."

The officer looked to have made the pec muscle under his badge dance, causing it to catch a beam of light. Cavanaugh couldn't help looking, but scrunched his brows together in disgust. The officer said something else, but Cavanaugh didn't hear him for trying to shake the vision of dancing pecs.

"A," the officer looked down at his notes. "Henry Childs gave us a call, claims he's an employee of yours."

The officer's statement had the inflection of a question, during which he made a secondary consult with the notepad he'd pulled from his pocket. The tall man, with long legs, had a pallid complexion compared to most who lived under the heat of the Texan sun. His partner, a few inches shorter, looked the part of a Texan, his skin boasting a toasty color indicative of the warm weather.

"Yes, he works for my family." Cavanaugh tried not to be snide.

"He said that your girlfriend had an accident and you brought her here."

Again with the questioning statement. Why wouldn't he just ask the questions instead of implying everything? Just as Cavanaugh was about to take a breath to answer the taller officer, his mother appeared behind them. His eyes settled on her for a second before either officer turned around. In that brief moment, she gave her head a subtle shake. The officers followed Cavanaugh's eyes to the woman who edged between them.

"Hi, son, I'm sorry it took me so long. How is she?" Cynthia asked, her tone laced with concern. A consternation that had not existed earlier that morning.

The familiar charade wasn't lost upon Cavanaugh. Cynthia, ever disquieted regarding the thoughts and opinions of others, often played the role, whether she liked the audience or not. She cherished her reputation and would do whatever it took to keep from tarnishing it, or the Jones' name.

"I don't know yet." Cavanaugh played along. "She's in surgery."

Cynthia had stepped between the two policemen and walked the few feet to Cavanaugh, throwing an arm around his neck and kissing his cheek. He almost rolled his eyes, but he didn't want to rouse suspicion among the two pairs that were watching them.

"I'm Cynthia Jones, his mother."

She extended her hand to the officers as though they were a part of a formal business meeting instead of a pending inquisition. Both men shook her dainty, frail looking hand, and introduced themselves as Officers Cooley and Pine.

"Mrs. Jones, we just wanted to ask your son a few routine questions," Cooley said.

They talked around Cavanaugh as if he were a nine-year-old boy who had no business speaking for himself. As though he should abide by the rule, 'children are to be seen and not heard.' She gave a curt nod and said:

"We'll be happy to tell you anything you need to know. Did Henry tell you we found her near the river? We think it may have been a riding accident, isn't that right, son?"

Cynthia gave Cavanaugh a knowing look. How she managed to contort half her face for this expression, he couldn't comprehend. The part of her face angled towards him held the expression, the other half looked passive, normal.

"Ma'am, if you don't mind, we would like to hear

Mr. Jones' recount of what happened this morning." The shorter officer, Pine, had found his voice.

"Sure, sure. My apologies." Cynthia's tone sounded about as casual as if she'd forgotten to give them sugar for their coffee.

"Mr. Jones, would you mind telling us what happened this morning to your girlfriend, is it?" Officer Cooley paused, checking his notepad again. Cavanaugh saw his eyes scanning the tiny page before flipping it over and back again. "Sarah...Evans."

Cavanaugh hated the way the officer said "girlfriend," his tone sounded teasing, skeptical.

"She's not my girlfriend, she's my wife!" he spat.

From the corner of his eye, Cavanaugh saw his mother flinch, but she didn't look at him. He knew it was a struggle for her to quell her reaction, not for his sake, but to save face in front of the cops. Cavanaugh, didn't care anymore about spilling his and Sarah's secret. Neither of them had ever mentioned their marriage to anyone. They spoke of it when they were alone together, thinking it would be better kept between the two of them, knowing that if their parents found out they would go ape shit— none more than the Joneses, and no one more than Cynthia. Cavanaugh knew, for sure, his mother would have an aneurysm if he had told her that he'd wed Sarah and without a prenup. Given Sarah's background, she would argue that Sarah had interest in Cavanaugh's money, the Joneses' fortune. It wouldn't be as much an argument as it would be Cynthia accusing Sarah of trying to enhance her standard of living.

Now, two years later, the secret between them had become commonplace, an inside joke that no one except Cavanaugh, Sarah and one other person were privy to. Well, not anymore.

"Sorry, sir, we didn't realize Miss Evans was your wife," Cooley said.

"She is my wife and her last name is Jones." Cavanaugh clenched his jaw as he spoke through his teeth.

Cynthia flinched again when Cavanaugh called Sarah his wife. Meanwhile, Cavanaugh made a mental note of each officer's badge number. A sober mind yielded his intelligence and amazing memory. Of course, that didn't happen as often as it should since he spent most days in some state of inebriation. However, considering how many of his brain cells he'd washed away with alcohol, seeing his sharpness and astute qualities was nothing short of remarkable.

"Got it. Sarah...Evans...Jones." Cooley scribbled on his pad while he spoke. "Can you tell us what happened?"

"There's not a whole lot to tell," Cavanaugh began. "I found her this morning in the wooded acre behind our fields, near the river with a black eye and bleeding. I put her in my car, rushed over here and handed her to the first doctor I saw."

Cavanaugh gave about as brief an explanation as Henrietta had when she'd updated him about Sarah's condition. The cops gave each other a look, their displeasure with Cavanaugh's lack of details obvious. Officer Pine gave a quick glance to Cavanaugh's shirt and then back to his face.

"I noticed you have some blood on your shirt there, Mr. Jones." Pine pointed at the smear in the center of Cavanaugh's chest. "Wanna tell us about that?"

"I was bored, so I cut myself with a scalpel while I was in here." Cavanaugh gave his mother and the officers a look of indignation. "I didn't have anything else to do." He paused. "What the fuck do you think! I just told you I found Sarah bleeding and carried her in myself. You guys are a couple of fucking idiots."

Cavanaugh threw the saturated words at them. The sting of the insult showing on the officers' faces.

"Mr. Jones, we're just trying to cover all the bases here," said Cooley.

"Well, why don't try asking questions that make some fucking sense! You wanna ask me some asinine shit about how I got blood on my shirt from carrying in my bleeding wife! Does that make sense to you? 'Cause it definitely doesn't to me."

"Honey, why don't you sit down." Cynthia placed a hand on Cavanaugh's shoulder and applied a little pressure. "Gentlemen, can we make this quick? This situation is stressful enough without any added aggravation."

"Absolutely," Pine answered.

Cynthia rubbed her hand up and down Cavanaugh's back. She put her arm around him and pushed down on his shoulder again. Cavanaugh snatched away from her and, instead of sitting down, he paced the floor again. He hadn't given any thought to how his actions may have been interpreted by the officers. Cavanaugh glanced at Cooley as he scribbled on his notepad. Averting his eyes to the floor, Cavanaugh took a moment to try to calm himself, trying to remain in a remote state of control.

"We'll move this along, just a couple more questions."

Cavanaugh didn't look up. He didn't care to be polite anymore, not that he had been.

"Mr. Childs said that Ms. Evans...er, Mrs. Jones is your girlfriend, but you're saying that she's your wife. Which is accurate?" Cooley asked.

Cavanaugh imagined his mother died a little death on the inside every time they referred to Sarah as his wife, while keeping her stoic poker face intact.

"I've told you, she's my wife," Cavanaugh said. Tiny death. "We've been married for two years." Another tiny death.

"Okay," Cooley dragged the word out a little. "And Mr. Childs didn't know about your marriage?"

"Yes, he knows, he just said that to fuck with you!" Cavanaugh couldn't control his tongue. "Obviously, fucking, not if he's calling her my girlfriend."

"Mr. Jones, could you please calm down?" Cooley asked.

"I'll calm down when you stop asking me stupid shit!"

The officers exchanged another look.

"How did you find her? I mean, how did you know to look for her in the woods behind the property and not elsewhere?" Pine asked the questions this time, his tone wavering a bit as if struggling to keep it steady.

"She loves to ride horses. Most mornings she'll take Casey out for a ride after she helps Mother with the others. We have plenty of space to ride, including the wooded areas, which are on the property, not behind it. It made sense to check the stalls and trails first."

"And who is Casey?"

"It's the fucking horse!" Cavanaugh threw his arms up in exasperation. "Casey's her horse! Where did you get your badge from, the Pic 'N Save? Geez, you are some dumb motherf—"

"Okay, officers. That's enough for now."

Cynthia cut off the rant of swears already making their way out of Cavanaugh's mouth. She ushered the men through the small doorway and out into the lobby. While there, she apologized for Cavanaugh's behavior and outbursts, promising to contact them later. Cooley gave her a card with various phone numbers on it, instructing her to call if Cavanaugh thought of something else or in case she needed anything. She watched them drive away and stalked back to the waiting room.

"You married her!" Cynthia may have kept her voice low but not the contempt out of it. "What were you thinking!"

"Ma, not now."

"Not now? Not now!" Cynthia fumed, but managed to look calm when she walked out of the waiting room and went to the nearest restroom.

When she re-entered the small space, she found Cavanaugh sitting in a chair talking with one of the nurses. Her face lost its angry tension when she saw the look on her son's face. She turned her gaze to the nurse, whose face seemed to match Cavanaugh's mood.

Henrietta had an arm around Cavanaugh's shoulder and spoke in a low whisper. Cynthia watched as Cavanaugh bobbed his head up and down but didn't look up from the floor. With a sympathetic rub of the back, the nurse rose to her feet, ducked past Cynthia's frozen form, and exited the room.

"CJ?" Cynthia called, her voice soft. Cavanaugh lifted his head, but his eyes remained downcast. "CJ?" she called again. He looked at her this time, his eyes dark.

CHAPTER SEVEN

Cynthia bridged the gap between herself and her son, but before she could sit, he sprang to his feet.

"I need a cigarette," he said, moving past her before her lips parted.

Cavanaugh made a beeline for the door, searching his pockets for his cigarettes and lighter. Coming up empty, he realized that he had not brought anything to the hospital that he would, on an average day, carry with him, including his wallet. He looked towards the car, wondering if he'd find the half pack of Virginia Slims in the console. He often kept them there and could always find a random matchbook from one bar or another somewhere in there too.

He went out to the car and just as he'd suspected, he found one pack of cigarettes containing two of the slim smokes and a brand new, unopened pack beneath it. He took the lesser pack, placed a cigarette between his lips, and dug around for a matchbook. He found one with two matches left inside and lit the stick at his lips, taking a long drag. He stared at the packaging, the image blurring and coming back into focus in short intervals. A chuckle escaped him when he thought of the way Sarah had always teased him about smoking Virginia Slims. She called them "girlie cigarettes," thinking they were such a vast contrast to his personality.

So, they were marketed for women, but Cavanaugh still liked them. He didn't consider himself a heavy smoker, and enjoyed the lighter tobacco and flavors. Sarah didn't like that he smoked, but she didn't grill him about it either. Out of respect for her, however, Cavanaugh would often enjoy his cigarettes outside, including when they were at home. The only time he smoked in front of her was when they were at the bar. For some reason, one he couldn't discern, smoking and drinking went hand in hand.

"Girlie man," she'd mumble every time he'd pull out one of the dainty cigarettes.

"I'll show you a girlie man!" he'd retort, often forgoing his cigarette to take up residence inside her. As a result, Cavanaugh didn't smoke as much as he once had. Thinking of that now, it seemed to be a sneaky little ploy of

Sarah's to get just that result.

"Sly little minx," Cavanaugh mumbled to himself, half a smile tilting his face.

He burned through about half of the cigarette before discarding it and returning to the waiting room. His mother was still there, though he wished she weren't. She yapped into her cell phone as though they were there for fun. She didn't look up when he walked in and didn't notice him standing there, so he turned around and walked away. He couldn't stand to be near her with her nonchalant attitude and feigned concern. Cavanaugh walked down the hall, scoffing at his mother's behavior. He almost collided with the doctor headed in his direction.

"Excuse me, sorry." Cavanaugh's eyes moved from the man's face to his hospital badge and back again. A tiny bit of light brightened his eyes as if the doctor was his one great hope. "Are you the doctor operating on Sarah Jones?"

"Yes." The doctor squirmed in Cavanaugh's grasp, his hands rather tight around his arms.

Noticing his discomfort, Cavanaugh looked from one of his hands to the other, clamped around the doctor like he was about to try to shake some sense into him.

"Sorry," Cavanaugh said again, yanking his hands off the doctor.

"I'm assuming you're family?" The doctor brushed

himself off.

"Yes. Cavanaugh Jones. I'm her husband."

The word "husband" sounded strange to his ears, tasted weird on his lips. He had never used the word, except in regards to the poor, miserable saps who'd exiled themselves to picket fences and attending juvenile sporting events. For certain, he had never used the term aloud as a reference to himself. Stranger than saying the word aloud, he liked it. He liked the way it sounded; he liked the odd taste it left in his mouth when he said it. The reason it didn't make his skin ripple with aversion, he suspected, had nothing to do with him and everything to do with Sarah. It validated his belonging to Sarah and her belonging to him, something he'd wanted, needed from the very beginning.

"I was just coming to speak with you, Mr. Jones." Cavanaugh nodded. "Your wife has sustained some pretty severe injuries. She has three broken ribs, multiple stab wounds, and a lacerated liver. She also has a cerebral contusion, which caused a brain hemorrhage. We had to relieve the pressure on her brain by..."

The doctor kept talking but Cavanaugh glazed over. He heard the man speaking, although he could not comprehend anything he'd said. Cavanaugh's mind ran in circles, thinking of all the pain Sarah had to be in, all the pain he couldn't relieve, all the pain he hadn't kept from her. He thought of how he'd failed her as a husband. He thought about the bastard who had done this to her and what he would do to him the moment he found his sorry ass. He thought…

"Mr. Jones?" the doctor's drone faded and his tone became more absolute, pulling Cavanaugh in again. "Mr. Jones? I said you can see her now. Just keep in mind that she is in a medically induced coma. We'll keep her that way until the swelling subsides," he continued. "Follow me, and I'll take you to her."

Cavanaugh hadn't the voice to speak. He just followed the man to the intensive care unit like an obedient child. The ICU wing had an eerie quiet. It lacked the shuffling, murmurs, and consistent movement of the other floors. The soft noise of beeping machines lay atop the blanket of silence while the hushed conversations between nurses and doctors floated just above.

Cavanaugh tiptoed across the shiny floors. Although he didn't mean to, he couldn't stop himself from doing it. He noticed because his eyes were trained on the floor, afraid to look at anything, anyone. As if looking would make the consequence worse than what he'd already come there for. Cavanaugh almost ran into the doctor again when he came to a stop outside of a room. A dry erase board, mounted to the wall just outside, read: Jones, Sarah with some other scribbles below her name.

The doctor didn't speak, neither did Cavanaugh, but

gave him permission to enter by extending his arm out and into the opened door. Without a word, Cavanaugh walked in, and the doctor departed, closing the door behind him. Cavanaugh noticed they'd put Sarah in a private room, something he appreciated.

He stood just inside the door, still staring at the floor, his shoes. At this point, they were one in the same. Cavanaugh wouldn't look, but he listened. He listened to the percussion of the ventilator as it forced air through the connecting tubes and into a pair of lungs. He listened to the whirling fans, cooling the many machines in the room. He listened to the sporadic beep of one device and the ticking of another. He listened to the unnatural breathing of the woman in the bed, his wife, he assumed, for he still had not looked at her.

He closed his eyes and raised his head from the floor. After a few beats, he fluttered his lids open, but turned away from the bed. He tried to give himself time. Time for what, he didn't know. On a heavy breath, Cavanaugh turned around and laid eyes on the woman in the bed for the first time.

Sarah looked worse now than when he'd found her. Tears smarted Cavanaugh's eyes, surprising him. A force pulled him to her bedside, feeling as though he wasn't taking physical steps, but gravitated toward her. Once there, he put a single finger under her hand like she was a newborn child. She looked so frail and breakable. A tear splashed onto the spot where their hands met. It took a few seconds for Cavanaugh to realize that the moisture had come from his eyes.

Cavanaugh sat in the chair next to her bed, staring at her, stroking the top of her hand with the pad of his thumb. Her skin looked thin and somewhat translucent. The tears in his eyes burned, making him uncomfortable in more ways than one. Cavanaugh had never been a crier. The last time he'd shed a tear he'd been eleven years old. While riding a colt, against the instruction of his parents, the horse had thrown him into the metal rails of the pen, breaking his arm in two places.

"I'm so sorry," he whispered.

Cavanaugh couldn't think of anything else to say. He wanted to trace the planes of her face the way always did, but he didn't, too afraid to touch her anywhere but her hand. She had tubes, needles and bandages all over. Bruises and stitches and scrapes. His eyes, still watery, skimmed her body and came back up to settle on her discolored, swollen eye, when the door to the room burst open. Cavanaugh whipped his head toward the loud bang, but not before swiping his sleeve across his face.

"Son, what the hell is going on?" Cavanaugh's father, Artemis, came into the room. "Oh, my God!"

Walking with a hunch, as though approaching a toddler, Artemis went to the other side of Sarah's bed.

Cavanaugh wondered why he walked that way; it wasn't his normal gait. Artemis took Sarah's hand. He didn't seem as afraid to touch her as Cavanaugh had been.

"Oh, sweet girl," he cooed as if he and Sarah were the only two in the room. "Who did this to you?"

Had Artemis not acknowledged his son upon entering the room, Cavanaugh would have wondered if he'd seen him at all. Art—no one ever called him Artemis, save for his wife when she was pissed at him—stared into Sarah's tumid facial features, stroking a patch of hair that hadn't been covered by bandages. He spoke in unintelligible murmurs as he pet and fawned over her, his eyes drinking her in as if he'd never seen someone so beautiful.

Art showed a fondness for Sarah from the day Cavanaugh brought her home to meet him and Cynthia. They'd forged an immediate kinship, often talking and laughing amongst themselves. Many mornings the two would have coffee together if Art hadn't left for one errand or another by the time Sarah made it to the main house. She'd stop there before heading to the stables. Sometimes she'd make breakfast for the three of them, herself, Art and Cavanaugh who often slept into the afternoon. Cynthia never ate breakfast, which meant Art never had the privilege, until Sarah showed up. She'd make his favorites, heaping his plate full of eggs, pancakes and bacon. After setting a plate aside for Cavanaugh, she'd seat herself at the table with him while he read the morning paper. Without asking, Art would hand over the funnies, which also held the puzzle pages she loved so much.

In quiet, they would eat and study their respective reading pages. Art expressed how much he enjoyed the morning company, never mind if they didn't talk the entire time. Sarah also enjoyed the quiet meal, the peace she wouldn't get if Cavanaugh were there with his loud mouth, brash, even in the waking hours of the day. When they were done, Sarah would wash the dishes and Art would dry. That's when the chatter started. Although Sarah had been close with her father, moments like the ones she'd shared with Art were a rarity, if they existed at all.

Gray had never helped with any chores and most of their conversations were about cars and engines. She loved cars and him, no doubt, but she more than welcomed the change. She and Art would talk about politics and its constant failure to the people it was meant to serve. They'd talk about horses and riding techniques, about school, food and relationships, including hers with Cavanaugh. If she had to choose a favorite topic to discuss, it would be food. Sarah, with her tiny frame, could out-eat Cavanaugh on a regular day.

Once their morning ritual ended, Art would head out to begin his day and Sarah would bring Cavanaugh's plate of food back to the pool house, setting it on the bar in the kitchen. She kept her riding boots at the door with a sock jammed into the pit of each shoe, often traipsing over to the main house barefoot. Sarah loved the feel of the cool grass dew on her naked feet. She loved the wet pavement stamping her soles with its moisture. Her first steps were always timid with anticipation of the cold liquid from either the heavens or the sprinklers. She'd always closed her eyes when she took her first couple of steps, standing on the tips of her toes before lowering her heels to the sod.

When Sarah had first arrived at the Jones estate, she took the time to get fully dressed before going to the main house, save for her shoes. Sometimes she wished she could just wake up and walk over the way Cavanaugh did, but that would be quite inappropriate since she preferred to sleep in one of Cavanaugh's shirts rather than a full set of pajamas. However, wearing shoes every minute of every day wasn't her thing. Her father deemed her preference for bare feet a bad habit, but she hadn't the desire to change that part of herself.

The first time Sarah crossed Cynthia's threshold devoid of shoes, the woman eyed her. Her clear distaste filled into the lines of her face. Although Sarah recognized the emotion Cynthia wore, she didn't see the need to explain herself, for she hadn't any excuse or justification for the act except to reveal that she enjoyed being naked and that did not exclude her feet.

Cynthia seemed to harbor an instant aversion to Sarah. When she walked into the house, Cynthia's eyes made a quick trip from Sarah's face to her scarlet painted toes—a color reserved for harlots, she'd voiced. Her gaze made a slower trek following the tattooed trail of stars leading from Sarah's little toe to encircling her ankle. Cynthia had met Sarah's face again with a raised eyebrow but hadn't said much. As time went on, however, she'd softened to the girl, but Art—Art became ensnared by her down-home traits straightaway.

Art often rambled about how delightful and refreshing he found Sarah to be. In fact, he'd laughed the first time he witnessed her menial but significant expression of freedom, her bare feet. He welcomed her distinction from the tarts and strumpets Cavanaugh, on other occasions, had woken up with, and he told him so. The women who wore too tall shoes and too short dresses, with their big hair and small minds. The ones who'd put on too much make-up and not enough clothes with greedy eyes and empty pocketbooks. Miss Sarah, as he sometimes called her, exhibited none of those traits, though she classified as the most meager of them all.

Art liked her. She didn't get wide-eyed when she witnessed their extravagances. She wasn't afraid to talk to him, and when she did, she spoke about subjects with depth. She wore battered jeans and flannel and jumped at the chance to help, undaunted when her hands got dirty or when she broke a nail. Most of all, she behaved like a daughter, rather than a guest, cooking and cleaning without being prompted or the promise of being paid. All that Art admired, Cynthia seemed to detest.

Sarah filled the emptiness that Art had, only once, admitted to having. He'd blurted out the sentiments of his partially hollow heart to Cynthia during an argument. Once CJ had grown past his toddler years, Art asked Cynthia about having more children. He wished for a daughter but Cynthia wasn't anxious for another child. After that, Art didn't press the issue. Instead, he would "misplace" her birth control pills. When she'd ask if he'd seen them, he'd deny knowing they existed at all. Despite his efforts, Cynthia never became pregnant, and their discussions about enlarging their family ceased altogether. By the time CJ reached adulthood Art transferred his latent dream to his son, expressing his desire to, one day, have a daughter-in-law. CJ tortured and killed his dream with every mess of a woman he brought home.

"I don't think this boy's ever gonna get married, let alone marry somebody decent," Art had said to Cynthia one night over dinner, but then came Sarah.

Now, the one respectable woman Cavanaugh had brought home lay in a hospital bed.

"I spoke to Dr. Easton on the way in about Sarah's injuries." Art said to Cavanaugh, still staring into Sarah's face. "What the hell happened, son? And why did he keep referring to Sarah as your wife, is there something I should know, CJ?"

Cavanaugh cleared his throat before speaking; but much like his father, he didn't look away from the frail figure occupying the bed.

"I don't know what happened to her. She was barely conscious when I found her in the woods by the river. I don't know who did this to her or who would want to. I can't imagine—" Cavanaugh broke off, still having not lifted his eyes. Speaking in a whisper, he continued. "I woke up in a pool of blood this morning, Dad. It wasn't mine; it was hers, so it couldn't have been just a bad fall from the horse. Besides, she's as good a rider as any of us and Casey is a good horse."

Art looked up at him, his eyes misty. His gaze shifted to various points on Cavanaugh's face, beyond him and then back to Sarah.

"Are you saying someone attacked her? Where— where in the Sam hell were you!" Art, spat the words at Cavanaugh.

"Ma didn't tell you? What did she say? Where is she anyway?" Cavanaugh asked, trying to avoid the questions because he felt too ashamed to answer them but Art wasn't distracted.

"Dammit, CJ! Answer me!"

"I was at home all right! Asleep." Cavanaugh bowed his head.

"Where was Sarah?"

"Laying next to me when I went to sleep, but when I woke up, she was gone and there was blood everywhere. I checked to see if it was me, but it wasn't."

"So somebody came into the pool house while you two were sleeping and what?"

"I don't know!"

"Dumbass, you were drunk again weren't cha?" Cavanaugh didn't bother to answer. "Now she's here, laid up in the hospital." Art shook his head and continued to stroke Sarah's hair.

"I know Dad, I know. I feel bad enough."

A long, quiet moment stretched between them.

"What's all this wife business?" Art asked, breaking the silence. "You wanna marry this girl? I must say it would be one of your better decisions. Let's hope she makes it through this if that's the case."

"I've already married her, Dad." The secret had come out, no use in trying to cover it up any longer. "The first day I met her." Cavanaugh gazed at Sarah. "Neil performed the ceremony."

"She's good for you, ya know. Sweet girl." Art cooed at her again when he said the last two words, having no reaction to the fact that CJ had just told him he'd married Sarah without telling him. "She gives you an air of responsibility, now if you could just lay off the fucking sauce!"

"You don't think I know that? You don't think I'm kicking myself for not protecting her! Someone came into our apartment and stabbed my wife and now she's here fighting for her life. You really don't think this is killing me? I love her, Dad. I've never loved anyone aside from you and mom, damn sure not like this. So save me the fucking lecture, I don't need it!"

Their exchanges were hushed yells, if there were such a thing. For a long while, neither of them spoke. During the silence, a nurse came into the room, checking Sarah's vitals and fluid bags. The palpable tension in the room seemed to render the woman silent. She nodded, mumbling a soft 'hello' before going through her routine. Neither Cavanaugh nor Art responded to the woman, their reddened faces and angry expressions acting as warning beacons. She moved with finesse around the room and departed without another sound. A wan smile served as her goodbye.

"Have you talked to the police yet?" Art turned to Cavanaugh.

"Yeah. Ma showed up right after they did."

"Where is your mother? Why isn't she here?"

"You didn't see her? She was in the waiting room."

"No, I haven't spoken to your mother since I left for Brady this morning."

"What?" Cavanaugh looked as if Art had just asked him the square root of pi. "How did you find out about Sarah?"

"Henry told me. When I pulled into the driveway at home, he ran headlong towards me. He looked like he was in shock which made me panic because he's always so calm. I didn't give him time to tell me everything or unload the two mares I'd hauled from Brady. When he told me Sarah was hurt and in the hospital, I threw him the keys to the truck, jumped in the car and sped over here."

"I can't believe Mom didn't call you. Henry called the police too; they came here to get my version of what happened. A couple of retards, if you ask me. They kept asking me dumb questions about shit I had already explained."

"Well, it doesn't take much to get into the academy anymore," Art said, sounding both serious and sarcastic. "I'm sure they were just doing their job, son. You're emotional, so everything is frustrating."

"Yeah, well, I still think they're idiots."

They sat for a while, watching Sarah's unmoving figure.

"Dad," Cavanaugh spoke in a low voice. "What are we going to do? How are we going to find out who did this?"

"I don't know, son. We have to start by letting the police do their jobs."

Cavanaugh didn't expect his father to have the answers, although he wished he had a better suggestion than relying on the cops. Considering the pair who'd paid him a visit earlier, their chances of finding Sarah's attacker, if left up to those two, were slim.

CHAPTER EIGHT

After a while, Art pulled himself from Sarah's side. He stepped a few paces backward, his eyes still resting on the girl. Cavanaugh had fallen asleep, sitting upright in his chair. He still had a single finger relaxed under Sarah's palm. Art reached for him, placing a hand on his shoulder but pulled back in almost the same moment he'd touched him. Art stared at his son, with a tilt of his head and scrunched eyebrows. Cavanaugh, although sitting straight up, was sound asleep. He didn't lean to the right, or left, forward or back.

"How in the hell does he do that?" Art half asked a nurse passing by. She stopped and peeked into the room where Art stood in the doorway. "My old ass would've fallen to the floor by now."

The nurse giggled, shrugging her shoulders, and

continued on her way.

Art left the hospital and headed home. He didn't see Cynthia on the way to the front doors, popping his head into the waiting room, checking to see if she were there, in case he'd missed her in passing. She hadn't come to the room to visit with Sarah nor had she called to tell him what had happened. Why hadn't she? Why hadn't she thought to call him or, at least, visit the girl? The questions were moot since Cynthia's behavior had proved contradictory over the years. Art had become accustomed to her odd way of dealing with things. When everyone else panicked, Cynthia became the voice of reason, but when it came to tiny matters, she'd become frazzled, up in arms. At funerals, she looked much too composed and pleasant for a mourner. When she'd lost her own mother, it wasn't just Art who found her temperament astonishing. While some others were inconsolable, Cynthia shook hands and smiled at one mourner after another, as if it were a social gathering rather than a funeral for the woman who'd given birth to her. Cynthia had also consoled other attendees. Who does that? Afterwards, she'd gone about her day as though she hadn't just buried her mother.

Was Cynthia concerned about Sarah at all? Would she so much as ask about the poor girl? Considering her previous conduct, probably not.

Art drove through the iron gates to their estate, following the snaking path that led to his private garage.

He clicked the button to open the automatic door and pulled the car into the space, cutting the engine before lowering the door. Looking around, Art's gaze rested on his truck, which he'd abandoned in such haste, parked in its rightful place along with the trailer. Henry had not just put it where it belonged but he'd washed it as well. The fading sunlight gleamed against the now shiny paint, where it had once been caked with mud and dust. All Art had left to do was take a shower and get dinner, thanks to Henry.

This particular garage sat detached from the house and the other garages. No one ever used it except Art, the one absolute space designated just for him. It held all the crap Cynthia wouldn't allow him to bring inside the house. In it were his hunting rifles, crossbows, fishing equipment and the like crammed into every available space and hung on the walls.

Art's collection of knives sat in a tall, slender area at the back of the garage. A third of them were just for show, being a quarter his age, the rest he used between his game and catch. Underneath the shelves displaying his knives, he'd installed a sink with hot and cold taps. Between the sink and the wall, he kept a folding table. The tiny cubby below was where he tossed his cleaning supplies and his chum bucket sat on the opposite side. Art had set everything up to make cleaning his catch as easy as possible. It also made it easy to deal with his wife, who could be a real killjoy when it came to Art and his other outdoor activities. She would cook anything he caught, but she didn't want to see or smell it beforehand. She'd insisted, more like demanded, the catch of the day be skinned, cleaned, gutted or whatever before bringing it inside. Art had also gone a step farther and bought a deep freezer, which he also kept in his makeshift man cave, for just such instances. He couldn't complain. This gave him the time and space to do what he enjoyed without the nagging of his wife in his ear, something that would take all the fun out of his extracurricular activities.

Art got out of his car and walked around the rear of the four-wheeler, which he also housed in his private garage. He looked at the body, caked with mud and other unidentifiable substances, and made a mental note to wash it within the coming week. Art walked to the door that led outside to a short walkway. Just to his left he'd put a clothes hamper and a rack for his shoes. He often changed before entering the house, saving himself the unnecessary grief of listening to his wife rant about him tracking this and that into the house. Art removed the boots he had been wearing all day and changed into soft loafers. When he entered the house, the aroma of pot roast greeted him, one of his favorite meals, coming in second to pancakes and bacon.

"Art? Is that you?" Cynthia asked from the kitchen.

"Yes, it's me." Art walked in and gave his wife a kiss on the cheek. "Smells good."

"Of course it does," she said, her tone smug, followed by an audible sigh.

"I'm going to take a shower; I'll be down in a bit."

"Ok, dear." Cynthia carried visible tension in her body, her movements looking stiff, her muscles rigid as she stirred the steaming pot on the stove.

Art stared at her back for a moment, but Cynthia didn't turn around. She didn't bother to ask about Sarah or Cavanaugh or his day. She went on cooking dinner as if it had been just any other day of the week. Art's stomach rumbled as he turned to go upstairs. He had not eaten much all day. His last "meal" had been a sleeve of peanut butter crackers, which he'd had early in the afternoon.

Walking into their grand bedroom, Art gazed at their king-sized bed and sighed. The room mimicked the rest of the house with its wooden furniture and inexpensive decor. The drapes were the priciest of decorative items, more expensive than their bed. The heavy tapestries, printed with odd-looking floral patterns, covered each of the four windows in the room. Colored a dark shade of olive green and tan, each fell into a tiny heap on the floor. Art, at first, couldn't understand why Cynthia had to spend so much money on cloth that just covered the windows.

"For all I care, we can cut some sheets and staple them up there!" Art had protested when Cynthia told him how much it would cost for the curtains.

Of course, she balked at his remark, all but saying 'I told you so' when the heating bill showed a drastic decrease once they'd been installed. Art later found relief in having them on the days where he'd been driving all night for one job or another and all he wanted to do was sleep. Pulling those heavy curtains closed blocked out most of the sunlight and made sleep come and stay easier.

Art, still stood gazing at the bed with its four wooden posts mounted on each corner. The comforter matched the drapes, which matched the sheets and the rug, all looked so inviting. Although, the precise matching could use a variant. He put a knee onto the edge of the bed, crawling his arms along the fluffy comforter until he hovered over the stack of pillows decorating the bed. He almost collapsed there, bending his elbows until his nose grazed the textured fabric on the printed pillow. He let out another sigh, but instead of falling onto the bed, he pushed himself up, slid off the bed and headed to the bathroom.

Art turned on the shower, allowing time for the water to heat to near scalding. He inhaled the steam as he undressed, tossing his clothes to the floor. Without releasing the cold-water tap, he stepped into the shower and slid the glass door shut. In their younger years, Art and Cynthia would shower together on occasion. That had long since ended. Besides that, the water temperature that Art used burned Cynthia's sensitive skin. How Art could stand in water so hot, let alone bathe in it for twenty minutes, was a bit disconcerting.

Art emerged from the shower boasting a shade of vermilion from the neck down. The splotches on his face picked up a varied shade of the hue. He scrubbed a large towel up and down his face, tousled his wispy hair, then dried the rest of his body. The towel he used joined the growing mound on the beige tiled floor. Standing in front of the wall-to-wall mirror, spanning across both vanities, Art spent a couple of minutes observing his physique. He took great care of himself and it showed. He looked pretty damned good for an old man. Just shy of the six-foot marker, Art had long sinewy limbs. His work and recreation kept his muscles well defined. His hair, though silvery and thinning, had not yet begun balding by any means. Art angled his head this way and that, his chocolatey brown eyes roved over his bushy eyebrows and large ears, which looked a little too large for his head, for anyone's head. Tufts of hair sprouted from his ears and nose, both of which he clipped at with an electric tool Cynthia had bought him for Christmas one year. Some gift!

After attending to his handsome features, Art walked away from his reflection to find something to put on. At the far right of their bedroom sat a pair of his and hers walk-in closets. Though Art could cite item for item what his closet held, he couldn't do the same for Cynthia's. He almost never ventured into her den of fabrics; for all he knew, she could have spell books and voodoo dolls in there. Of course, he didn't care much to know.

Art stepped into his closet and opened several drawers of a chest made of unfinished wood. Sifting through the drawers, he closed each one with a bang until he got to the last one at the bottom. There, he paused before pulling out two articles of clothing. He could never remember where Cynthia put his things or which drawer she'd designated for what. Sometimes Cynthia would just lay out clothes for him as if he were an eight-year-old child dressing himself for school. He never protested, saved him the trouble of looking for himself and leaving his closet in a state of disarray. Art's wardrobe wasn't extensive or complicated. It consisted of jeans and button-down shirts, most of which were varied shades of plaid. He owned a whopping three suits—two of which still had the tags on them—and a single pair of dress shoes.

Art donned a pair of flannel pajama bottoms and a plain white t-shirt, leaving his feet bare, reminiscent of Sarah. Maybe she'd rubbed off on him. Sadness descended upon Art as he thought of the way Sarah's eyes twinkled when she peeked over the top of a newspaper while she did her crossword puzzles. He thought it the cutest thing how she'd look around the room, just over the paper's edge, as if the answer to the crossword clue were hidden in the room somewhere. A wan smile pulled at one corner of Art's face but fell the second he thought about her condition.

Art shook his head and turned to walk out of the

closet, headed towards the door to go downstairs. Just as he stepped out into the hall, he made an about face back to the bathroom to gather his discarded clothes. As he scooped the pile up from the floor, a glint of silver flashed, catching his eye. He squatted down to his heels and peered under the vanity. At the base, he saw a metal object incongruous with the spotlessness that Cynthia thrived on maintaining throughout the house. Art picked up the object, holding it between his forefinger and thumb.

He recognized the item right away. The sharp, metal shard belonged to one of the knives in his collection. However, it didn't belong to a knife he ever used, making it more of an oddity that part of it had ended up in his bathroom. It came from a piece he took out just to admire and, on occasion, to polish as not to lose its luster. Its thin blade, serrated on both sides, had once been quite the apt tool, but given its age, Art knew its susceptibility to breakage. He'd never thought of testing its durability, figuring himself lucky enough to own such a treasured piece. Anger burned his face at the thought of someone rifling through his knife collection and grew hotter at the reality of his prized knife being ruined. The original blade, about an inch and a half long, had a sharp, piercing tip. He held the tip between his fingers, eyeing the jagged edge where it had been broken.

His bones creaked as he raised himself to standing. Art continued to stare at thing between his fingers for a few more seconds until he heard the doorbell ring. He pulled his eyes away from the shard in his hand, placed it on the counter top and dashed to the top of the stairs. He never picked up his clothes.

"Cynthia! Don't you open that door!" Art shouted, trotting down the stairs in a hurry.

"What? Why?" she asked, still walking towards the front door.

"Cause there's somebody loose out there hurting our family. That's why!"

"That girl's hardly family," Cynthia mumbled under her breath. Despite her low tone, the words found Art's ears just the same.

"She's a Jones now. That makes her family!"

Art pointed a stern finger towards the floor, as if punctuating his sentences. His tone oozed with irritation, every word dripping with displeasure at Cynthia's disregard for Sarah.

How Cynthia still hadn't warmed up to the girl baffled anyone who'd met Sarah. She, after all, had been a constant presence over the past couple of years. Her sweet nature and willingness to help were easy things to love, not to mention the fact she extended that courtesy to Cynthia despite the woman's apparent disdain for her. Apart from that, the girl never asked anything of or from them, and that included Cavanaugh.

The doorbell rang again and then again as Art stood looking at Cynthia. Without another word, he went to a closet just right of the front door. He sifted behind the long rack of coats until he touched a double-barreled rifle. Wrapping his hand around the cold metal, he slid his hand down the barrels, almost as if he were caressing it. His fingers glided over the intricate engraving until he tightened them around the stock. He kept the gun loaded, counting on that as he pulled it from the closet, flicking the safety off with one hand and using the other to open the front door. Cynthia had retreated a few feet back, half-hiding behind a wall. She peeked out as Art pulled the door open.

A figure crouched in the darkness, the porch light casting eerie shadows upon him. Art had the rifle in his hand, the dim light creating a twinkle on its metal.

"Dad," Cavanaugh said, as he stood up and leaned against the doorjamb. Art let out a sigh.

"Shit, boy! You almost got yourself one! Where's your key?" Art relaxed his grip, pushing the safety back on with his thumb.

"I don't have it. And since when do we lock doors around here, anyway?"

"Since this morning!"

Cavanaugh slid past Art into the foyer.

"Put that thing away," he said, pushing the gun aside with the back of his hand.

Art shut the front door after taking a quick look outside, not that he could see a whole lot in the darkness, and returned the gun to its hiding place.

"I left everything in the apartment this morning when I took Sarah to the hospital. The car key was in her purse and that's all I had with me. That's what I came back for." Cavanaugh walked through the foyer toward the kitchen. "I don't have my wallet or anything and the pool house is locked, I need the key."

Cynthia was already rummaging through the kitchen drawer where they kept all the spares.

"How is she?" Art asked.

"The same. I just snuck out so I could come get my wallet and phone. I need to hurry back. I'd hate for her to wake up and I'm not there."

Cavanaugh and Art had strolled to the doorway leading to the kitchen, by then Cynthia had met them there with the key and a Tupperware dish she'd filled with pot roast, rice, and green beans. She handed the dish to Cavanaugh.

"Thanks Ma." She kissed his cheek and walked

away.

"What's her problem?" Cavanaugh asked.

"You know your mother," Art said. "She never reacts as expected." Cavanaugh shrugged his shoulders. No denying the truth. "Call me if there's any change."

"I will. Thanks for coming by today."

"I'll come by in the morning."

With that, Cavanaugh turned to leave.

"CJ?" Art called. When his son turned around, he said, "I'm here for you, kid, both of you. You know I love Sarah like a daughter, and I'm glad to have her as one."

Cavanaugh nodded.

"Thanks, Dad."

He walked out the door and crossed the dark, wet lawn to the home he shared with Sarah. He dreaded having to enter the apartment, all the more, without her. It wasn't often they didn't come home together or where one wasn't already home, waiting for the other. He knew a horrid scene awaited him on the other side of the door. A reminder of what had befallen her. He braced himself, as much as he could, to revisit the scene he had left this morning.

He put the key in the lock and turned it, his

movements slow and apprehensive, feeling each click as it moved out of place. On an exhale, he pushed the door open.

Cavanaugh had imagined there would be crime scene tape and evidence of police proceedings all around the apartment. He had a pretty vivid image of CSI in his head, expecting the apartment to look something like what he'd seen on the show. However, that wasn't the scene. What he saw turned out to be something altogether different. He scanned the room, remembering the broken pair of glasses that he'd put on the breakfast bar, but the glasses weren't there anymore. He took slow steps toward the bedroom, expecting to see the mess he'd woken up in.

Astonished, Cavanaugh stood frozen in the doorway. Upon the bed, tucked, ironed, and pulled taut were a fresh set of sheets and new comforter. The blood on the floor had disappeared, and the room no longer smelled of iron, but instead like laundry detergent and disinfectant. Dazed and confused, Cavanaugh could do nothing but stand and look around the room. Shouldn't there be yellow tape and fingerprinting dust on every surface? Shouldn't there still be cops lingering and gathering clues? That's the way it happened in the movies. Had to be some truth to that, right?

Cavanaugh, so stricken by the cleanliness of the

apartment, had almost forgotten why he'd come home in the first place. His eyes made an invisible trail from the floor to the nightstand closest to where he stood and then to the other. Each had been cut from an aged oak tree, making them heavy as shit. Cavanaugh knew because he had moved them into the pool-house himself. The store where he had bought them didn't offer delivery services, something he did not understand.

The logs were stained dark, a perfect match to Cavanaugh and Sarah's wooden bed, causing the grooves and divots on the tables to stand out. Instead of being sanded to a smooth finish, the ridges and rings of the wood had been exaggerated, providing a tangible and visible texture. Perched between two ridges were Sarah's favorite glasses. When Cavanaugh saw them sitting there, he tilted his head to the left and scrunched his brows together.

He reached his hand out as he stepped toward the table, expecting the glasses to fall to pieces the moment he touched them. To test the theory, he flicked the frames with a single finger and waited for them to dismantle, but they just tumbled backward, completely intact. What the hell? Cavanaugh thought. He knew he had crushed the lenses under his boot that morning. He remembered swearing, having imagined what Sarah's reaction would be.

Cavanaugh squinted at the glasses as if waiting for them to get up and fly away, or disappear in a plume of smoke. When neither of those things happened, he picked them up and examined them closer, opening and closing the temple arms, turning them around and upside down in his hands. They were in perfect condition, too perfect. Cavanaugh looked back to the nightstand. He'd been so bewildered by the glasses that he hadn't noticed his wallet and cell phone with the charger sitting there, inches from Sarah's specs. Cavanaugh had come prepared to search for those items, but there they were, in a logical place. The phone and its charger right next to one another with the charger's wire coiled around itself, as if it had just been removed from its store packaging. Convenient, yet puzzling. Nevertheless, he grabbed each item, shoved them into his pockets, and went into the bathroom to get his toothbrush and Sarah's—for when she awoke.

In the bathroom, Cavanaugh yanked his and her toothbrush from the medicine cabinet and a tube of toothpaste. As he slammed the cabinet shut and turned to leave, he caught a glimpse of the bath in the mirror's reflection, noticing the shower curtain had been replaced. He thought of the saturated sheets he'd left in the tub, wheeled around, and yanked the curtain open. Empty. Clean. The tub all but sparkled. All that was missing were twinkling stars in corners of the basin and a chiming sound effect. This had to be Cynthia's doing. The freakishly neat woman cleaned nonstop. It's like she had a disease, bordering on obsession.

Growing up, Cavanaugh often found himself annoyed by his mother's compulsive tendencies. She lived in a constant state of housekeeping. She refused to hire anyone to help keep the house tidy, not because they couldn't afford it or because she didn't want the help. Her argument:

"They won't do it the way I will," she'd say. "I'll just go behind them and redo it anyway. What's the sense in that?"

That proved to be true the time or two where someone had tried to help, infuriating Cynthia. Just as she'd said, she went behind them and readjusted, refolded and rewashed what had been touched. Then she'd clean all the things they hadn't bothered as well. The dust buster may as well have been an appendage. She had vacuumed CJ with it once when he'd come in from outside dirtier than what she could stand, which meant any dirt at all. Cynthia had run the hand held vacuum up and down CJ's body, sucking his shirt and shorts into the mouth of the machine. When she couldn't get him clean enough, she made him strip at the door and sent him straight to the bath. She'd thrown his clothes in the garbage bin outside, never bothering to find out if there would be any benefit to washing them first.

CJ waited for the day when his mom would hose him down in the yard, instead of making him disrobe at the door. That, he looked forward to, but that would have been too much like fun. Something Cynthia was not.

Shaking free of the reminiscent thoughts and earlier visions of the day, Cavanaugh headed for the door with his full pockets. He double backed, having caught a glimpse of his stained clothing, and decided to change. Replacing all the items he'd come for in the pockets of the clean clothes he'd put on, Cavanaugh headed for the door once more. He turned and looked at the neat space, wondering about his mother, wondering how she'd done it, and if the police had told her she could. He didn't linger long. He had to get back to Sarah, dealing with his mother would have to wait.

CHAPTER NINE

The next few weeks went by in a blur of Styrofoam cups, tar-like coffee and catnaps in chairs. The nursing staff had been nice enough to put a cot in Sarah's room for Cavanaugh to sleep on, although he could sleep anywhere, in any position. Sometimes to relieve the tension in his back, he afforded himself the luxury of lounging on the cot, but not often. He didn't feel he deserved any comforts while Sarah lay in a state of forced unconsciousness.

Cavanaugh couldn't decide if he believed it or not, but he'd heard the debates between scientific and spiritual minds that, although in a coma, the unconscious could still hear. He'd never had to make the choice, but in case the latter were true, he spent his days having one-way conversations with Sarah. He talked and laughed as though she were awake and interjecting her own thoughts and diatribes.

Art, on the other hand, made no secret that he believed Sarah could hear every word they spoke. He visited almost every day, speaking to her in soft murmurs, encouraging her to wake up, to help him with the crossword puzzles. He sat with her and tried to do them as well as she did, asking her what she thought the answer could be to twelve across or thirty-one down.

"I miss you, sweet girl," Art whispered. "I miss our morning ritual. Breakfast, puzzles, our little talks."

Cynthia's idea of breakfast was coffee and she wouldn't take the time to have a cup with him. She'd brew a pot and leave a mug next to it for Art to make as he liked. She probably didn't know how he took his coffee. Before Sarah, Art spent his mornings alone at the breakfast table sipping his hot drink as Cynthia paid more attention the steeds in the barn. Sarah had warmed his empty mornings, and he preferred her unresponsive company to Cynthia's cold demeanor first thing in the morning.

When Art visited Sarah, he'd walk into the room with his cheerful disposition and force CJ to go home and shower. Cynthia had stopped by a time or two but had never come into the room. She'd summon one or both of them to retrieve the meal she had brought. Either that or she would just leave it at the nurse's station. She had no problem making sure her men ate, but seemed to care nothing at all about the girl. She didn't talk about, ask about, or mention Sarah, not so much as an acknowledgement of her existence. CJ and Art were beyond trying to understand Cynthia or her actions. They let her carry on without a word from either of them.

Within the passing weeks, each Jones, apart from Sarah, of course, had been questioned, on more than one occasion. It seemed the investigators were trying to trip them up in the possibilities of suspected lies. Each one of their accounts of the morning remained the same. The investigators, at last, moved on, but nothing seemed to come of the evidence they'd gathered—or lack of. It turned out that they had given Cynthia the okay to clean the apartment, a fact which quelled Cavanaugh's musings about his mother's neurotic cleaning habits.

Back in Sarah's room, Cavanaugh sat in a chair next to her bed, babbling about a vehicle in the Car and Driver magazine he'd been thumbing through for the past thirty minutes. He had his nose so far in the book that he hadn't noticed when Sarah's hand twitched. He licked his thumb and pinched the corner of the page, staring at it for a moment longer before flinging it to the other side of the book. The paper crackled as he continued to ramble, his eyes skimming the words and lingering over the images. Meanwhile, Sarah's body moved for the first time on its own. Cavanaugh, mid-chuckle, looked up from his magazine for a moment, and then back to his bright, colorful pages. He often did this to engage her, though she lay motionless and unresponsive.

This time, however, was different. It took a few seconds for Cavanaugh to register that Sarah had, in fact, been moving when he looked up. He yanked his head up and his hands went limp causing the magazine to fall to the floor. Too stunned to do much else, he watched, his fear escalating as a twitch of Sarah's hand progressed into convulsions throughout her entire body. Paralyzed by the scene, he watched her muscles turn from flaccid to rigid as she bucked on the bed. Cavanaugh rose from his chair in slow-motion. He heard her gagging on the tube in her throat while the machines connected to her body escalated their hysteric beeps. He couldn't think clearly enough to press the call button for the nurse; instead he threw himself on top of Sarah, covering her slight body with his in hopes of keeping her from hurting herself or pulling out any of the tubes or lines which looked to be everywhere.

"I need some help in here!" Cavanaugh yelled, throwing his voice towards the hallway through the half-opened door. "Somebody! Please!"

Cavanaugh turned back to Sarah, readjusting himself as she writhed beneath him.

"Sir, we need you to move!" someone said. Cavanaugh hadn't realized anyone had entered the room and though he'd heard the command, he couldn't move fast enough. "Now!"

Before Cavanaugh could pull himself off his wife, someone yanked him up and slung him towards the door. He stumbled as he tried to regain his balance. Within seconds, the room teemed with medical personnel. They filed in, bumping and scooting until they'd succeeded in pushing Cavanaugh to the outside of their circle. He couldn't see Sarah anymore, but he could hear the clamor of voices and movement. One person yelled instructions over one shoulder and then another, while the others complied. Cavanaugh, despite his height, couldn't see over the huddle of people working on Sarah. He stood on the tips of his toes trying to get some sort of view of her, but he couldn't, he couldn't do anything but listen. He tried to count the beeps on the machine that tracked Sarah's heart rate, but there were too many and they came too fast for him to keep up.

"Sarah, it's okay, honey." Cavanaugh heard a woman speaking to her in a calm voice amid the chaos. "We're going to remove the tube from your throat, okay?"

He felt helpless, useless, standing in the corner as everyone tended to Sarah while he just watched. He found it hard to stand still, so he shuffled from one foot to the other. He fiddled with his belt buckle and jingled the keys in his pocket. Standing on his toes again, he hoped to see over the hub of people surrounding her, but to no avail. Just when he thought he'd reached his breaking point, he noticed the beeping had slowed and the urgency in the room subsided. One by one, each uniformed professional straightened to an erect position, trailing out of the room in a totter of soft-soled shoes and starched fabric.

"Good news, Mr. Jones." One doctor had remained behind to speak with Cavanaugh. "Sarah's breathing on her own now. She started fighting against the breathing tube; that's what all the commotion was about. She still can't talk yet, however. Her throat will be sore for a while."

Cavanaugh nodded, turning away from the doctor to look at Sarah. He couldn't stop bobbing his head, whispering under his breath as if trying to convince himself that the doctor's words were true. The man gave Cavanaugh a pat on the back before leaving him to his murmuring.

Sarah's eyes were wide as she stared at Cavanaugh. He could almost see question marks forming in her pupils, but he stood frozen in place, awash with several emotions, each fighting for prominence, for recognition, for dominance. Her gaze then moved from his and darted around the room. Sarah's eyes seemed to have held him in place. The moment they left him, he moved. In one long stride he reached her and knelt at her bedside.

"Babe," his voice came out in a timid whisper.

He couldn't manage to say anything more. Sarah stared at him, her eyes shifting back and forth, once again holding him in place. They sat for a long while, looking at each other until Sarah's eyes became shiny with tears.

"No, no, no, babe, don't cry, please." He tried to soothe her, but in truth, he needed soothing as he fought his own set of tears. "Please, don't cry, please. It's okay, I'm right here."

He rested his head in Sarah's hand which lay palm up on the edge of the bed. He let out a long breath as he worked to keep himself from falling to pieces in front of her. He felt relief, sadness, happiness, joy and fear all at the same time, making it difficult to get a handle on any one thing. He wanted to laugh, cry, yell, run. He wanted to both cradle her like a baby and crush her in a bear hug. He didn't know what to do, or which desire to give in to.

Cavanaugh wasn't an emotional man. He wasn't much of a feeler at all, but this woman refuted everything he thought he was and contradicted all that he swore he wasn't.

His forehead became warm from her touch, something he relished so much in that moment. With her thumb, Sarah ruffled a few strands Cavanaugh's hair. Then, as if ordering each finger, she caressed his skin. Her touch felt like ecstasy. That tiny action was all it took to press latent tears from Cavanaugh's eyes. He'd been staring at the floor and now watched each droplet as it sailed to the ground, ending in a soundless splash. He allowed himself a few tears which almost seemed not to exist because he couldn't see them, each one becoming an unnoticeable part of the linoleum.

Pressing an index finger and thumb into his eye sockets, he tried to do away with the wetness. When he trusted himself to look up, he lifted his head. Sarah had not moved anymore and she'd closed her eyes again. For a moment, Cavanaugh feared that she'd slipped back into the dark abyss from which she'd just awakened. His assurance came from listening to the consistent beeping that monitored her heart and watching the rise and fall of her chest, no longer forced by a machine. Sarah's soft breaths came and went unassisted.

"I'm so sorry, love. I'm so sorry," he whispered.

While Sarah slept, Cavanaugh pulled his phone from his pocket and dialed his father's cell instead of calling the house, in an effort to avoid his mother. He'd rather leave his dad to relay the message to her.

"Dad," Cavanaugh said into the phone after a couple of rings.

"Yeah, son. Is everything all right?" Art's voice weighed heavy with sleep, prompting Cavanaugh to check his watch.

"Sorry, Dad, I didn't realize the time, but I had to call and tell you that Sarah woke up. They took the tube out of her throat and she's breathing on her own."

"That's wonderful. Let me put some clothes on. I'll be right over."

Art sat up and threw his legs over the side of the bed. Moonlight streamed through the windows allowing him to see most of the bedroom, including his wife who slept beside him, undisturbed. Art's gaze trailed the room until it landed on a neat display of his clothes. He pushed his fist into the mattress and pushed himself about halfway up when Cavanaugh responded.

"No, Dad, just wait until the morning. She's gone back to sleep." Art took a breath to say something but Cavanaugh didn't give him the chance to speak. "I think they gave her more sedatives to keep her calm. Come in the morning and bring the crossword from the paper."

A small smile pulled at the corner of Art's mouth as he lowered himself back onto the bed. He sighed.

"Ok, I'll see you two in the morning."

Art hung up the phone, but couldn't go back to sleep after getting such good news about Sarah. He looked over at Cynthia, who hadn't changed positions, and placed a gentle kiss on the tip of her nose before inching out of bed. He tiptoed around the room, grabbed a few things, being as quiet as he could, and went down the stairs into his private garage.

Once there, he went over to his knife collection and chose a 1973, 120 buck hunting knife. He pulled it from its weathered, leather sheath and inspected it. He ran his finger along the blade and gave it a light tap on the tip, admiring it for a moment longer before replacing it in the holder and clipping it to his belt loop. Then, Art changed from his house slippers into his work boots and put on a ball cap, pulling the bill down low.

In a few more smooth moves, a characteristic which Cavanaugh had inherited, Art loaded his hunting rifle and mounted it to the front of his ATV. He stashed a small box of bullets in a case strapped to the vehicle. After securing his weapons, he went over to the garage door, released the lock latch, and heaved open the metal door in lieu of using the automatic opener. He turned the ignition to the ATV, listening to the engine's quiet hum. It seemed a vehicle like it would make more noise but, on mornings like these, it was a good thing it didn't. He backed out of the garage, hopping off the ATV to pull the garage door closed and drove into the woods to see what he could shoot and kill.

"Not a bad way to start the morning," Art said aloud.

A few hours later Art returned with a nice-sized fallow tied to the back of his vehicle. He smiled to himself as he drove back to the house, a look of pride on his face. By now the sun had risen and Cynthia would be in the kitchen or making her way to the stables, as usual. Though she didn't know about Sarah yet, and perhaps didn't care very much, the news warranted celebration. Sarah's awakening meant she'd gotten one step closer to recovery. The deer Art had caught would make a great celebratory meal and Cynthia made a mean venison stew.

Art pulled into the garage, taking out the folded table he kept by the sink, his chum bucket and a few other things he needed to set up his station for skinning and cleaning the deer. He went through the motions with expert precision, working with such method and meticulousness that he didn't seem to think much about any movement or task. A skilled knifeman, hunter, archer and rider, Art made the outdoors his business and he made a point to be good at it, if not the best. In a matter of minutes, he'd finished with the deer and began to break down his makeshift station and sanitize the area. He placed the flanks of meat into an ice filled cooler to take inside.

He washed and wiped each surface he'd used and then moved on to wash his ATV. He had to put his back into it to remove the caked on grime, mud and blood from his morning hunt. It had been so long since he'd washed it, the mud had dried in hard clumps. The morning had been a dry one, as had mornings before but the last time he'd taken it out had to have been a wet day from the looks of it.

"Remind me not to let mud dry on this thing again," he grumbled to himself. "Because trying to get this off sure is a pain in my ass!"

By the time he got the body of the vehicle in satisfactory condition, he'd been too nettled to bother sluicing the muddy tires. Instead, he parked it in its designated spot to let it air dry and began polishing his knives.

Art chose and polished each knife with a soft cloth and a delicate touch. One at a time, he pulled the knives from their sheaths, polished them and replaced them. The very last knife was the most dated knife. With steady, tactful hands, he slid the blade out to rest on a fleecy fabric. He counted the serrated prongs on either side as he removed it. He knew the exact number of prongs, just as he knew each nick and scratch that covered the hilt of every knife he owned. If he were the one who'd marred the knife, he could tell you how it happened and when.

"18, 19, 20," Art counted aloud, but his counting should not have stopped at twenty.

There were twenty-four prongs on either side, but he had no more to count. The last inch and a half that included the final four prongs was missing. The tip of this knife had a sharp point, smoothing out after the twenty-fourth prong. He pulled the knife all the way out of its cover and stared at the broken metal, confused and a little pissed. Knives don't break themselves and he'd never use this particular knife given its fragility.

"Dammit!" He banged his fist on the table, still holding the sheath in his hand.

A piece of metal tinkled as it fell onto the table. The shard of metal from his prized blade lay there just as it had on his bathroom floor. He stared at it for a moment, squinting his eyes. His gaze travelled to points in the garage and then back to the remnant of his broken knife.

"What the hell? How did this end up in my bathroom and then turn up in here?" He mused.

It was clear he'd forgotten about the find, but the more he stared at it, the more evident his anger became. Blood rushed up his neck, coloring his face with its heat. Art stalked into the house, without changing his clothes or shoes.

"Cynthia!" Art marched into the kitchen. "Cynthia!"

Everything in the house was fair game except for that garage. He'd deemed it off limits and more, the things inside it. Art called for Cynthia several times, receiving nothing but his echo as an answer. The quiet, however, gave him a moment to think somewhat clearer.

"Cynthia," he said again, this time to himself.

He ran up the stairs to their bedroom and stood in the doorway, looking around from one piece of furniture to the other. Then, he made a beeline for the dresser and began searching through Cynthia's drawers, rummaging through them one at a time. He pushed clothes aside, sifted through her underwear, and shook out her folded garments. She'd unleash a tirade later for the mess he was making. He shoved another drawer closed, but it bounced back a little. He shoved it again, but it wouldn't close.

Art knelt down and peered over the rim of the drawer, looking to see if he could find what kept the drawer from closing. Sure enough, wedged between the side of the drawer and its track he found something. He reached in to pull the paper from the crevice, ripping a piece of it in the process. In his hand, he held a crumpled picture, its dark image brooding from the worn paper. The eyes of the subject, made red by the camera's flash, looked a little blurry to Art but then again, he didn't have on his glasses.

He dashed over to his nightstand, yanking the drawer open, to retrieve the specs he kept there. He found the case, but not the glasses, just its cleaning cloth. For as long as Art had been wearing glasses, he still had a hard time remembering to bring them wherever he went. Instead, he bought several pair and kept them in places he frequented like in the drawer of his nightstand, in the glovebox of his truck, in his overnight bag.

"Where the hell are my glasses?" he asked the empty room.

Slamming the drawer shut, Art squinted hard

at the image, trying to make out the figure with the red eyes. He saw that not only were the eyes red, but there also seemed to be other splotches of red in the photo. Art held the picture within an inch of his face, willing his pupils to focus.

"Is that S—" he couldn't get the name past his lips.

The phone rang. Art started, but he didn't take his eyes away from the picture in front of him. When the shrill sound of the ringer pierced the quiet again, he moved toward the phone. He picked up the receiver, moving in slow motion while he continued to stare at the picture.

"Hello?" Cavanaugh's voice prompted him on the other end. "Dad, is that you?"

Art held the phone to his ear, but had not yet spoken. His breathing changed, sounding a bit labored as it came out in short huffs. Cavanaugh knew the sound. Anytime his father got the slightest bit upset his breathing was the first indication of his foul mood.

"Dad, are you okay?" Cavanaugh paused, waiting for an answer. "Dad!"

"Yeah," Art responded.

"What is going on?"

"Uh, what? Nothing, son. Just got back from hunting. About to, uh, change and head over. How is she, how's my girl?"

Cavanaugh noticed his father trying to sound casual, but he wasn't fooled. The line went quiet but Cavanaugh could still hear his father's rapid breathing.

"Don't change the subject, Dad. What's going on?"

Silence. Cavanaugh called to his father a few times but Art didn't answer. After a few moments, Cavanaugh became annoyed and hung up.

"Hello?" Art, still holding the phone to his ear, spoke into the receiver, although the line had gone dead. "Hello?" Nothing.

Art looked at the phone as it blared a busy signal. He lowered the receiver from his ear, dropping it onto its cradle. He had not heard Cavanaugh's responses to his questions and didn't bother calling him back. He'd be at the hospital soon.

"I don't want to tell you what I found," he whispered, as though Cavanaugh was in the room. "Hell, I don't believe it my damn self! Don't trust these failing eyes of mine. It's probably not what I think anyway. There's no way. It can't be who I think it is," he continued to mumble to himself as walked down the stairs.

Could the person in the photo be a stranger

covered in animal blood from hunting? Perhaps the red streaks are paint? It was possible, but the eyes, pleading to the camera's lens for help, pleading to the person behind it were a unique pair.

Art returned to the garage, hid the photo away and removed his soiled clothes and shoes. He took a quick shower, dressed, and stopped in the kitchen before heading out the door. On the counter sat a mug of coffee and a covered dish filled with last night's dinner. He opened the refrigerator, sifted through the containers on the shelves but closed the refrigerator door without retrieving anything. Art turned and grabbed the covered dish to take to CJ, and took a sip of his coffee before going out to his truck.

CHAPTER TEN

Well on his way, Art looked over at the passenger seat where he'd sat the dish of food. He scrunched his brows together.

"Dammit!" He banged the heel of his hand on the steering wheel. "I forgot the paper."

He stopped at a convenience store about a block from the hospital and picked up one. By the time he'd arrived at St. Luke's, Art's mood had visibly elevated. His morning find seemed to have been pushed to the far corners of his mind. He walked through the automatic doors of the front entrance, whistling a tune. He walked with the gait of a child, all but skipping down the corridor, smiling, nodding and chatting with the nurses he'd come to know. He approached Sarah's room, still whistling, but before he made it to her door, a commotion erupted.

"Honey, what's the matter?" CJ's voice floated out into the hallway. "Babe, calm down. Nurse Watts!"

Art stood, stock-still at the opening of the door, he didn't go inside. He didn't look inside. Art, as unrealistic as it seemed, expected everything to be harmonious; for Sarah to be awake, talking, smiling and laughing. He'd expected to hear her adorable laughter wafting out into the hallway like the smell of fresh baked goods, not the voice of his son in a panic because something was wrong with her.

A nurse rushed past him, trailing behind her the mixed scents of industrial cleaners and flowers. Nurse Watts, perhaps, although he didn't get a look at her. Art stayed in place, quiet, listening as the room's occupants talked, soothed, and worked to ensure Sarah's wellness. At a point, the clamor died down and quiet took its place. Subdued murmurs replaced rushed instructions; the whir of machines and monitors, once again, became audible. Nurse Watts, an average sized woman with long, braided hair and skin the color of a dark roast coffee, emerged from Sarah's room.

"Mr. Jones?" she said, her island accent altering her words, as she placed a gentle hand on Art's arm. She moved into his direct line of sight. "She's okay. She just got a little startled, that's all. She may have had a flashback of her accident, yeah?" Nurse Watts didn't wait for Art to respond, but nodded her head up and down as though he had. Art mimicked her, nodding his head in compliance.

"Go on," she urged. Although, the way she'd said it sounded like, g'won.

Art took slow steps, sliding his feet toward the door, peeking into the room before taking a step inside. Cavanaugh sat by Sarah's bedside as he always did but didn't turn around when Art came in. Sarah looked at Art standing in the doorway and her eyes widened. She didn't speak but her mouth pulled upward at one corner around the edge of the oxygen mask that covered her nose and mouth. Art smiled at her, watching as the clear plastic fogged and cleared with her every rapid breath she took. She stared at him, prompting Cavanaugh to turn around.

"Hey, Dad, I didn't hear you come in."

"My girl," Art crooned, as if Cavanaugh hadn't said a word.

"Well, hello to you too, old man," Cavanaugh said, his tone terse. "What's up with you today? Are you making a game of ignoring me?"

"I'm sorry son, I haven't meant to. Just a little overwhelmed is all." Art stared at Sarah as he walked closer, taking a moment to give his son a pat on the back.

"Join the fucking club. How do you think she feels?" Cavanaugh's annoyance with his father's behavior resonated through his words. He turned his attention back to his wife and whispered to her, "We've missed you."

Sarah looked at Cavanaugh, her mask tilting up on one side again, bigger this time. Lifting her hand, she stroked his stubbled cheek. Cavanaugh leaned into her touch, closing his eyes, and reveled in the feel of her hand on his skin. He had not shaved in a few days, knowing how much Sarah liked his beard scruffy and unkempt. Again, Art moved closer, pulling up a chair to sit down. The chair screeched against the floor as he dragged it closer to her bedside, piercing the quiet. Sarah started, jerking her eyes in his direction.

"Dammit, Dad!" Cavanaugh snapped. "Could you make some more noise? I don't think the coma patient heard you downstairs! You're scaring her!"

"Sorry," Art raised his hands in a gesture of surrender. "Your mother sent you some leftovers."

"Couldn't bring it herself, huh?" Cavanaugh scoffed. "Coward," he mumbled under his breath. "Did you tell her that Sarah was awake?"

"No, she was asleep when you called. I didn't wake her. By the time I got back from my hunt, she was already gone. I suppose she knew I'd be coming here today, so she left this out."

Cavanaugh grunted. He took a breath to speak but when he laid eyes on Sarah, he closed his mouth and smiled at her, instead.

"I'm going to warm this up while you visit with Dad, okay, baby?" Cavanaugh leaned into Sarah and nuzzled her jaw with his nose, placing a shallow kiss on her neck. "I'll only be a few minutes. You can do the crosswords together."

Sarah had said just a few words since she'd awakened. She and Cavanaugh communicated with their eyes when she couldn't find her voice. Her eyes went wide again and she gripped his hand, locking her eyes on his. Sarah's heart rate began to rise, her mask fogging with her short, quick bursts of breath. Cavanaugh looked at the monitors, having learned to read them from spending so much time there. He looked into her eyes for a long moment and realized she didn't want him to go.

"I'm not leaving the building, babe. It's okay, Art, will be here. Right, Dad?"

Cavanaugh turned to his father who nodded his agreement, in lieu of speaking. Cavanaugh turned back to Sarah, trying to reassure her with his eyes, but her expression hadn't changed. The numbers on the monitors climbed and, quiet as it was, Cavanaugh could still hear the low click Sarah made in the back of her throat. She made a single click and that had been enough for Cavanaugh.

"Seej," He peered into her eyes as he reached up to stroke her hair. "Relax, baby, I won't leave. I'm here. I'm not going anywhere, okay?"

Cavanaugh held her gaze and after a while, Sarah let out a long sigh. Her pulse made a slow decline as Cavanaugh rubbed the pads of his fingers and thumb over her hairline. He noticed a light perspiration on her temples. He reached over with his free hand and grabbed a couple of tissues from a box which sat on a rolling tray nearby. He pat the tissues across her forehead and down around her ears. Sarah closed her eyes on another exhale as her breathing calmed and although she didn't let go of Cavanaugh's hand, she relaxed her grip, allowing it to lay limp on top of his. Her eyes resumed their normal shape and her drooping eyelids lost their flushed red color as she calmed.

"You're getting all worked up over nothing," Cavanaugh whispered to her.

Art watched the way his son dealt with Sarah. CJ had never spoken with such softness, such mildness to anyone, not even a child. He had always been brash, unrelenting and unapologetic of his tongue. Sarah had a softening power over him, a gentle persuasion. Art stared at Cavanaugh, staring at Sarah as her eyelids closed over her eyes for longer and longer periods of time, until she'd fallen asleep.

For a time, Art and Cavanaugh just sat there watching Sarah sleep, much like a parent watches their sleeping infant. Cavanaugh couldn't bring himself to let Sarah's hand go, for fear that it might wake her, fear that she'd think he'd left. So, he twisted in his chair to face his father, intending to ask if he'd mind heating up the food he'd brought for him. However, the chair Art had been sitting was empty. To Cavanaugh's chagrin, Art had left and taken the bowl of leftovers with him. He'd been so stealthy that Cavanaugh hadn't heard him get up or walk out of the room. He swore under his breath as his stomach made protests of its own.

Cavanaugh found it harder to leave for any length of time, now that Sarah was lucid. He lay his head on the edge of the bed, his forehead against Sarah's arm, and closed his eyes. He had difficulty reopening them because he hadn't slept all night; instead, he'd spent the night in a constant state of watch. He didn't want to miss when Sarah would awake again, which she had done several times.

A few minutes later Art walked in and set his cup down on a nearby table and tapped his son on the shoulder.

"Huh!" Cavanaugh's head snapped up from the bed. "What's wrong?" He didn't realize he'd dozed off.

Cavanaugh looked around, panicked, but when his eyes settled on Sarah, who slept undisturbed, he relaxed.

"Shh, shh, shh," Art warned. "You'll wake her."

Art had snuck out of the room to the cafeteria and warmed his coffee and Cavanaugh's food. He extended the bowl to his son and pulled a packet of plastic silverware from his pocket.

"I warmed your food. You've got to be starving by now." Art handed Cavanaugh the silverware.

"I am. Thanks. I thought you'd left. I just put my head down for a second."

Cavanaugh had slept for a few minutes, but it felt like half an hour. He didn't feel refreshed, but he did feel a difference. Slipping his hand from beneath Sarah's, Cavanaugh popped the top off the dish, and dug in. He shoveled the food into his mouth, one steaming heap at a time, sometimes two. He ate as if chewing were a waste of time because he wasn't taking the extra time or energy to do it. Art finished his coffee in silence and made yet another feeble attempt at doing the newspaper's puzzle without Sarah. After eating, Cavanaugh put his head down again, unable to help himself. Within seconds he fell asleep again, evident by his soft snore. Again, Art tiptoed out of the room and headed down the hall. This time he did leave, walking out of the building to his truck.

A little over a week later, officers Cooley and Pine showed up at St. Luke's hospital again. They'd been keeping a close eye on the Jones case and an even closer eye on the Joneses...all of them. All the pieces to the Jones puzzle hadn't quite fit and the ones that did weren't a perfect match. Cooley and Pine had been monitoring Sarah Jones' condition and had gotten word that she'd awakened, but they didn't question her right away. They were cops, but they weren't insensitive, at least not all the time. Besides, they'd been stonewalled by Cavanaugh before, slowing the investigation. There were enough unanswered questions for that to happen again on its own.

Pine approached the nurses station, taking a minute to converse with the nurses about Sarah and her visitors before going to her room. Cooley had gone ahead of Pine, making three soft raps on the door labeled: S.E. Jones, Dr. Wettig, Nurse Watts.

"Yeah," Cavanaugh answered.

With a soft click, Cooley pushed the door open, just enough to peek his head in.

"May we come in?" Cooley asked in a soft, but firm tone.

Cavanaugh wasn't happy to see the officer, not because he didn't want to find who had hurt Sarah, but because Cavanaugh thought this specific officer and his partner were a couple of dumbasses. Despite that, Cavanaugh gave a simple nod and Cooley walked in. Officer Pine had already caught up with him and followed him in, closing the door behind himself with a faint click.

"Hello, Mr. and Mrs. Jones," Cooley spoke first, introducing himself and Pine, who just nodded in agreement.

It took a minute for Cavanaugh to digest the way they'd addressed him...and Sarah. It may as well have been a wedding introduction to Cavanaugh because it was the first time anyone had addressed them as a unit, a married couple. Sarah, awake and alert, gave Cavanaugh a perplexed look when they'd come in and that look turned to shock when the officers called them both Jones.

"It's okay, babe. We've been exposed, it's not our little secret anymore," Cavanaugh gave her a wink.

"Do you mind if we ask you a few questions?" Cooley asked.

Cavanaugh gave another nod and they began asking Sarah basic questions: name, address, identifying the person next to her. She got two out of three correct. Sarah had been talking more and more each day, losing the rasp caused by the breathing tube that had been in her throat. She had not yet returned to her high energy self, but some of her sparkle had pushed its way to the surface. Seeing her smile again excited Cavanaugh most, he'd missed it. Her laugh, however, he missed more.

"Do you know what happened?" Cooley asked. "Why you're here, in the hospital?"

Sarah looked at Cavanaugh again, just as she'd done every time one of them asked her a question, as though he were her answer key. For all the answers she didn't have Cavanaugh would give her pats of reassurance. She shook her head, no. Prior to this, Cooley and Pine had instructed Cavanaugh not to tell Sarah too much about the circumstances of her hospital stay; good thing too, because he didn't have the heart to do it anyway.

Sarah had told Cavanaugh how confused she felt, waking up in a strange environment, and worse, that strange environment happened to be a hospital, of all places. Since she hadn't been sick in years, it had been a daunting discovery to wake up among the stark walls and plastic-covered beds. Such a cold change from the warmth of home with her familiar things and Cavanaugh sleeping beside her, his body pressed against hers. Sarah told him how much she'd missed the simplest things: sleeping on her belly, for one. The smell of store-bought detergent versus the industrial strength brand that lacked the additives she loved. Most of all, she'd said, she missed Cavanaugh's scent. She missed the way it lingered in vacant spaces after he'd long left the room. In this place, Cavanaugh's smell seemed to be swallowed by sterility.

After being prompted, Sarah told them about the last morning she could remember, relaying the events aloud for the officers. Cavanaugh had no idea what she did or didn't remember, he'd never asked. As she spoke,

Cavanaugh filled in the words Sarah couldn't seem to find. The officers discouraged him from helping her, but he ignored them.

According to Sarah, the morning of the "accident" started much the same as all her other mornings on the Jones estate. She'd gotten up just before dawn, a bit earlier than normal for her, and headed out into the darkness on her way to the stables. Most mornings, she and Art would have breakfast together, but he had to go to Brady, Texas, about two and a half hours away.

"When I got to the stables Cynthia was already hard at work. I'd forgotten my glasses, but I decided to help feed the boarders first. Then I gave Casey a brushing, tacked him and led him across the field to the pool house so I could get my glasses. I didn't tie him up because I knew I'd only be a second.

I creaked the door open and stepped over this one." She pointed a thumb at Cavanaugh. "He was asleep on the floor, right where I'd left him. I didn't bother closing the door and tiptoed inside, though there wasn't much need to be quiet, Cavanaugh sleeps like the dead. I could probably go marching through our apartment with drums and cymbals and it wouldn't wake him." They all chuckled. "I grabbed my glasses from the nightstand and made my way back to the door. I was holding my glasses in my hand, but jumped when I saw someone standing in the doorway."

Cooley and Pine looked at each other while Cavanaugh's eyes stretched wide as he looked at Sarah.

"Did you recognize this person?" Cooley asked.

"No, I couldn't really see. It was too dark."

"Can you tell us anything about this person? Could you tell if it were a man or woman?"

"Anything you can remember will help," Pine chimed in.

Cavanaugh looked as if his life depended on the next words out of her mouth. He leaned into her, squeezing her hand while he waited for her to answer. Sarah looked at him for a moment and then looked back at the officers. She gave a small shake of her head. Cavanaugh closed his eyes and sighed.

"Is something wrong, Mr. Jones?"

Cavanaugh flinched at Cooley's voice as though he'd been pinched.

"Aside from the obvious?" Cavanaugh barked.

Sarah spread a confused look between each officer and Cavanaugh.

"Mrs. Jones? Can you tell us anything about the person you saw? Were they short or tall? Thin or wide?" Pine had a notepad in his hand, his pen poised for details.

"I—I don't know. Tall, I guess. I'm pretty short, so most everyone seems tall to me." She grinned.

"Could you tell if this person was thin or heavy?"

Sarah shook her head again.

"Ok," Cooley said. "Well, can you tell us what happened next? Did the person speak to you, did they say anything?"

"I don't remember."

"What did you do when you noticed him standing there?"

Cavanaugh turned to look at Cooley who gave him a condemning look.

"She said she didn't know if it were a man or woman, why are you saying him?"

"It's just a general term, Mr. Jones."

Cavanaugh turned back to Sarah with a shake of his head.

"Mrs. Jones, what did you do when you saw him in the doorway?" Cooley asked again.

"Well, I jumped because I didn't expect to see anybody there."

"And you don't remember them saying anything?"

Pine asked.

"No."

"What about you, did you say anything to them?"

"Yeah," Sarah giggled. "I said, 'Oh, shit!'"

"And why did you say that?" Pine looked up from his notepad.

"Because I was surprised."

"Were you afraid?"

"No."

"And then what happened?" Pine scribbled away on his tiny sheets of paper.

"I laughed because I felt silly. I mean, who else would be on the property at such an early hour other than the people who lived or worked there? I had no reason to be afraid."

"Then what happened?" Cooley shifted his weight to one foot.

"That's all I remember."

"You don't know what happened after that? Nothing else?"

Sarah shook her head for a third time.

"What's the very next thing you remember?"

She looked at Cavanaugh. "Waking up here." Her tone went flat, the sadness evident in her voice.

Pine took note after note and urged Sarah to elaborate as much as she could. However, the memory wasn't there. She couldn't recall anything beyond what she'd told them. She seemed to have no idea that Cavanaugh had found her in the woods.

Cavanaugh would rather her not remember anything. He felt almost relieved that the incident wouldn't be a part of her lasting memory, and therefore, an invisible nightmare.

The officers murmured amongst themselves while consulting Pine's notes.

"You did good, baby." Cavanaugh kissed her hand.

With her free hand, Sarah fiddled at her neck.

"I did?"

"Yeah, of course, you did." Cavanaugh smiled and moved his gaze from her eyes to her nervous hands. "What's wrong? Are the tubes bothering you?"

She didn't answer but kept fiddling, running her hand across her chest and then behind her neck.

"Where's my necklace?" Sarah turned to him, her eyes wide and glassy like child asking about a promise she'd been made.

Cavanaugh looked at her neck, although he knew he'd just see the tubes intertwined there. The simple piece of jewelry, made up of a fragile golden thread, held a small charm of an equine jumper. She wore it all the time and, in that moment, Cavanaugh remembered how she would always toy with it.

"I don't know but we'll find it."

Pine asked Sarah to describe the necklace after asking Cavanaugh if, perhaps, the hospital staff had removed it.

Not long after, the officers gave each other a quick nod and prepared to leave, putting away their tiny notebooks and pens. Although, the questioning hadn't lasted very long, it proved too much for Sarah. She'd fallen asleep before the officers had the chance to excuse themselves. Cooley made a gesture to Cavanaugh, motioning for him to step outside of the room. He followed the officers to the door.

"So, what do you think? I know she didn't remember much, but does any of that help?" Cavanaugh asked.

"Mr. Jones," Pine began. "Do you mind if we

search your property again?"

Cavanaugh looked at him, wondering what he'd written in his itty bitty notebook.

"With the information your wife has given us, there may be some new leads to explore."

"What do you mean? Like what?"

"We can't be sure just yet, but we'd like to take another look around, make sure we haven't missed anything."

Their reticence annoyed Cavanaugh. He felt as if they were hiding something. He wanted to say no just to spite them, but Sarah's suffering wasn't worth such a trivial victory. The true victory would be finding the person who'd hurt her. If Cavanaugh couldn't exact his own revenge he should let the cops point the perp out, it would make it easier for him. So, Cavanaugh gave his consent for them to search the property again. He'd have to leave it up to Henry to deal with the police because Cynthia wouldn't be there. She and Art were transporting a few horses and also stopping in Abilene to check on the station, something Cavanaugh would do on a regular basis, but Sarah held the trump card and nothing was more important to Cavanaugh than Sarah.

Cavanaugh had never felt for any other human the way he did about Sarah. He often felt pangs of ambivalence regarding his emotions, ever since the first day they'd met. Even now, he both loved and hated the idea of this searing emotion within him. He wanted to guard and protect her; to find her assailant and kill him with his bare hands; to love her and coddle her as though it would be enough to heal her physical wounds. He didn't care as much about himself anymore, except to be wherever she was. He knew that made her happy. These were the thoughts that allowed Cavanaugh to say yes to the idiot cops who he hoped were, at least, smart enough to find what they needed to catch the offender.

"Would it be okay if we went now?" Cooley asked. "While she's asleep, you could escort us over."

Cavanaugh turned to look into the room at Sarah, who'd fallen into a deep sleep. Still, he couldn't concede to the idea of leaving her.

With Cavanaugh's back to the officers, Pine gave him a subtle 'what-the-hell-are-you-doing' look while Cooley returned the expression with a smug grin. He gestured for Pine to follow along and mouthed something to him but Cavanaugh turned around before he could finish. Cooley placed the stern look he always kept back on his face.

"I'm not leaving her," Cavanaugh said, his voice calmer than it had ever been. "My parents are out of town, but Henry is there. He works the farm. I'll call him and tell him to let you in."

"Thank you, Mr. Jones. We appreciate your cooperation."

Sarah stirred in her bed, garnering Cavanaugh's attention at once.

"I know you want to get back in there, but would you mind signing this for me." Cooley retrieved some papers from an invisible shelf, it seemed, handing them to Cavanaugh. "This just gives us written consent for the search." Sarah stirred again.

"Yeah, yeah." Cavanaugh didn't waste time reading the words on the page before scribbling his name on the form.

"Okay, Mr. Jones, we'll—"

Before Cooley could finish his sentence, Cavanaugh dashed back into Sarah's room, sitting in his designated chair at her bedside.

"That went better than I thought it would," Pine said as he and Cooley walked through the main lobby and out the front doors. "I was certain he would give us all kinds of hell."

Cooley didn't speak, instead, he responded with a mischievous smile as he slid behind the wheel of the police cruiser. The officers had already cleared Cavanaugh as a suspect, but they had other persons of interest to pursue. In less than an hour, the Jones estate teemed with uniformed men and women, meticulous in their search of the property. Cavanaugh's suspicions were spot on in thinking the police were withholding information, because they were, and now they were combing the wooded area behind the estate again, including the river's edge.

Cooley also instructed the team to search the main house, despite the fact that they already had, watching as a team of individuals picked through the elder Jones' master bedroom. The other bedrooms in the house were spotless, without wrinkle, looking more like starchy hotel rooms than bedrooms in someone's home. The Jones' bedroom looked just as clean, but more lived in. Now, their drawers and doors sat open from Cooley and his team's inspection. The officer took slow steps around the room, peering into, around and under things as others performed their tasks.

"Hey, Cooley," two techs called in unison. One stood near a tall dresser, the other in the master bathroom.

"Just a sec," Cooley answered, throwing his voice towards the bathroom.

He walked over to the dresser and stood next to the thin man holding a pair of tweezers, between the tips of which he held a ripped corner of a picture. There wasn't enough of the image to guess at what it might be a part of, but Cooley instructed them to bag and keep it anyway.

"Keep looking and see if you can find the rest of that photo. Check the sides and the rear of each drawer and don't forget about the base."

He walked towards the bathroom while he belted out his orders to everyone in the room. Standing in the doorway, he scanned the space, waiting for the other tech to reveal his find. Then the man said the phrase just about everyone used when they think they've found something big:

"Cooley," he paused. "You need to see this."

CHAPTER ELEVEN

Sarah sat up in bed, laughing at her husband. It wasn't odd to think of him that way; however, acknowledging him as such aloud would take some getting used to. So would hearing people refer to her as Mrs. Jones. Their secret, now common knowledge, their inside joke, wasn't just theirs anymore. It appeared that while she slept Cavanaugh had made an announcement to the world. She had to admit, she felt relieved that his parents knew about the true status of their relationship. It made her feel less like a bimbo and more like a part of the family, whether Cynthia regarded her as the same or not. She couldn't understand why the woman still had such a profound disdain for her. Sarah had tried to cultivate a relationship with Cynthia by using their love for horses as a medium, hoping that helping in the barn would be the common interest they could bond over. It hadn't worked.

Cynthia, though always cordial, would tell Sarah what she needed done and continued with her own tasks, almost as if Sarah weren't there. At first, Sarah could more or less appreciate Cynthia's wariness towards her; after all, she had grown up in a trailer. While Sarah wasn't poverty stricken, according to national statistics, compared to them she was piss poor. She had gone to public school and worked at a chain store. She'd never attended college and she'd come to Texas on one of their buses with nothing but a backpack and a perforated dream.

Sarah came to the Jones estate young, naïve and, to Cynthia's overt disapproval, bound by law and love to her sole offspring. The single heir to their fortune. Sarah knew she'd been one among many women Cavanaugh had paraded around town with. However, this time she had attained the coveted title of wife, while the others had not reached the status of girlfriend.

At least Art had a fondness for her. She knew, without doubt, that he liked her, loved her. It felt good to have a sober father who cared for her and took care of her more than she did him. She missed Art and wondered why no one else ever came to visit except Cavanaugh, although thankful to have him. She looked at Cavanaugh, feeling lucky that he'd chosen her. Sarah had had her fair share of days when she didn't feel so lucky. Today wasn't one of them. Sitting in a hospital bed, she still counted herself blessed to have such an uxorious husband. He, without fail, occupied the space, both in the infirmary and in her heart, filling the openness with a bliss she had not had the guts to dream of finding. Cavanaugh had not been a part of her dream, nor had a life in Texas, but a dream devoid of any of those factors now would be deemed a nightmare.

Sarah stared at Cavanaugh as he rambled about some hilarious—at least to him—event that had occurred during his college years. She watched the way his face crinkled and his eyes lit, noticing a few gray hairs along his hairline. She wondered how long they'd been there because she didn't recall them being there before. Then again, she couldn't seem to remember much as of late. Cavanaugh talked and talked, while keeping hold of her hand. Sarah looked down at where his hand held hers and using her thumb, she stroked the top of one of his fingers. She smiled, looking up at him, tickled that he hadn't noticed because he'd been so focused on keeping her entertained. Perhaps he wanted to entertain himself, she couldn't tell. Not that it mattered either way, seeing as it was working.

Sarah dropped her gaze to her left hand, willing one of her fingers to move. She'd been having mobility issues with her left side. While the doctors were astounded by her recovery and progress, Sarah found herself more frustrated with her limitations. Although she favored her left hand, she didn't feel a complete debilitation because she'd always been ambidextrous, but that didn't alleviate her frustration. She couldn't decide which felt worse, lack of mobility or lack of knowledge.

Sarah still didn't know how she'd ended up in the hospital and since no one would give her a straight answer, she'd stopped asking. Instead, she gleaned clues from hushed conversations, not that it had done much good. She concluded that she'd been in some type of accident, which is how they always referred to anything in relation to her trauma. She assumed she had been thrown from a horse, but of course, she couldn't remember being on one in the first place. At least not that day.

"Mrs. Jones?" There was that name again.

A nurse stood in the doorway. Sarah eyed the wheelchair she'd pushed in, knowing what it meant. It meant she had to go to a physical therapy session. It also meant she'd have to leave Cavanaugh because he wasn't allowed to accompany her. However, Sarah took great comfort knowing that he would be sitting in the lobby waiting for her. That he would be there, standing guard. She felt protected but still wished they'd let him to come with her.

❧

Cavanaugh smiled when Henrietta called Sarah by her married name. He'd warmed to the term. He liked having a 'Mrs. Jones', no matter if his mother hated it. Something about that made him smile, though he wasn't sure why. He wished his mother would at least try to like Sarah. It wasn't as if they didn't get along, because they did, but that was about as far as it went. Cynthia granted her courtesy, nothing more.

"Sarah, I told you to call me Sarah." Cavanaugh looked at Henrietta as Sarah responded to her name. "Although, I will say, I like the sound of that."

"I know," the nurse replied. "That's why I said it."

Cavanaugh had become very fond of Henrietta. She'd cared for Sarah since he'd brought her in. He liked that she could go from no-nonsense and feisty to soft-hearted and sensitive in a matter of seconds. It seemed most medical professionals, along with their required anatomy classes, took a seminar on detachment and desensitization. Henrietta must have skipped that seminar because she radiated warmth.

"Are you ready for your physical therapy session?" she asked Sarah.

"Do I have a choice?"

"No." Henrietta wheeled the chair closer to her bed.

"So why did you ask?"

"Because I like crushing your dreams!" Henrietta's broad smile underlined her words. "Come on, princess, your chariot awaits."

Both women laughed and Cavanaugh joined the chorus. Henrietta pushed the chair up to Sarah's bed. Cavanaugh moved his chair out of the way and helped Sarah swing her legs over the side. Then he helped Henrietta get her into the chair as they took turns making jokes about one thing or another, the same way they always did. They'd made a ritual of it all. Cavanaugh knew Sarah's therapy sessions lasted about an hour but he'd hated when they'd told him he wouldn't be allowed to accompany her behind the double doors. Restricted, like all the other family members, he had to bide his time in the waiting room.

"Hey, Seej," Cavanaugh began, leaning down to speak into her ear.

Sarah looked up at him with wide eyes. He'd almost forgotten how beautiful her eyes were, losing himself within them for a moment. Bursts of copper streaked from her pupils but the perimeter of her irises were a soft shade of sea green. When she touched his hand it drew him out of his trance.

"Um, uh, I'm going to run over to the house and take a quick shower, okay? I'm starting to offend the nurses." He grinned.

Cavanaugh didn't want to leave her, but he had held off bathing for as long as he could. In truth, he hadn't just begun to offend the nurses, he'd begun to offend himself.

"I'll be back before your session is over. Promise." He looked into her eyes again. "I love you."

The last few words came out of Cavanaugh's mouth in a way that felt accidental. His face twisted as if it itched, as though he couldn't be sure who'd said the words. Cavanaugh wasn't the lovey-dovey type. He didn't go around spouting sonnets and writing love poems. He trusted all the people he loved knew he loved them, whether he said it or not. Of course, it wasn't the first time he'd said 'I love you' and not the first time he'd said the words to Sarah. Yet, something about it, the way he'd said it, the emotional stir that happened when he'd said it, felt different...more intense, almost painful.

"You too, cowboy," Sarah responded, her tone close to her usual fire and spark.

Cavanaugh felt drawn to her, her energy reeling him in like a fish on a line. Just as pointless as it would be for a hooked fish to fight against the pull of the line, he would be likewise ineffectual in his strivings to resist her. Without contemplation, Cavanaugh pressed a firm but gentle kiss on Sarah's lips. They hadn't shared a kiss since the night before this nightmare began. Cavanaugh, afraid to touch her, would allow his lips but a whisper at her hands or bare arms, but nothing more...until now. In the moment, Cavanaugh couldn't help himself. Sarah leaned into him, lifting her hand up to his neck. The sensation of her touch, her lips, felt all but new to him. He felt so aware of their points of contact. Had it always felt this way to be close to her? he asked himself and then answered his own question in the same thought. Only when I'm sober. He had never been sober for this long of a stretch, not in years.

When Cavanaugh pulled away from Sarah, the seconds stretching ahead like minutes, both their eyes were glassy.

"Never mind me!" Henrietta fanned herself. "Whew!"

She'd retreated to a far corner of the waiting room, in an effort to give the couple a moment of shallow privacy. She pulled her braids up and fanned her neck as she walked back to stand behind Sarah's wheelchair. Sarah giggled, her cheeks ruddy, as she put her fingers to her lips.

"Henrietta," Cavanaugh cleared his throat. "Take care of my Mrs."

"Not to worry, Mr. Jones. I wouldn't do anything less."

"I think it's okay if you call me Cavanaugh, now."

She smiled and nodded. Cavanaugh thought he saw a glistening in her eyes, but couldn't be sure because of his own glassy vision. As she wheeled Sarah down the hall, Cavanaugh heard Henrietta gush about how lovely she thought the two of them were.

He, headed in the opposite direction, made time by jogging across the lacquered floors and tarred parking lot to his car. He slid in behind the wheel, but before he pushed the button to liven the engine, his eyes caught the shiny, silver loop of Sarah's purse strap. Her bag, still on the floor, sat tucked just under the front of the passenger's seat. He hadn't noticed it there after all this time and hadn't given it any thought when he'd sent Henry to have the car detailed. Cavanaugh pulled the bag up by the handle and plopped it onto the seat, making a mental note to take it inside when he got home.

A few small items spilled onto the seat and floor. Cavanaugh swept the items on the seat back into her bag, not bothering with the items that had fallen to the floor. He glanced at them, deeming them little less than important and decided he'd pick them up later. That is, until his eyes saw something that should not have been there. He stared at the object, reaching for it in slow motion. He took a closer look at it, perplexity lining his face.

"What the—" he began.

His voice filled the quiet of the car's cabin, making what should have been a soft remark, sound loud. Cavanaugh held the object between his index finger and thumb; he didn't want to touch the bloodstains that coated it. His eyes grew wide and his stomach churned the moment he thought of who it might belong to. He threw the item on the seat in disgust, as if touching it burned. He wasn't sure what to do, his mind awash with possibilities and implications, but no rationale. He sat there, staring out the front window, a bevy of thoughts swirling round and round, dizzying him.

At some point, he pulled a business card from his rear pant pocket, but he sat there, staring at it. He read and re-read the name, address, and phone number on the card. He looked at the fuzzy corners and tiny places where the lettering had faded from whatever friction the card had encountered. After a while, Cavanaugh pulled out his cell phone and punched the number in.

"I'm looking for Officer Cooley," Cavanaugh said into the phone, foregoing any type of greeting. He paused before continuing, not waiting for a response, but waiting for the words he needed to say to present themselves. "...or Officer Pine. Either will do."

"Just a moment. I'll patch you through," said the woman on the other end.

A few seconds later Cavanaugh heard the recorded voicemail for Officer Pine. He hung up and dialed the number again, asking for Cooley. The woman gave the same response as she had before and patched Cavanaugh through. He listened to the phone ring, counting each one, waiting to hear another recorded message, but it never came. He heard the line connect and an extensive fumbling of the phone receiver before someone spoke: "Officer Cooley."

Cavanaugh went silent, frozen while he held the phone to his ear. He disconnected the call. His breaths came fast, one breath would come so fast on the heels of the last, it's a wonder he hadn't hyperventilated. Drops of sweat made a path through the maze of his hair down to his hairline. He concentrated hard to compose his thoughts, but it didn't seem to be working very well, in part because he didn't want to think about it...any of it. He just wanted Sarah to get better, come home, and her attacker to pay the price for fucking with the Joneses. Thinking of that made him pick the phone up for the third time and call the officer's phone number.

"This is Cooley."

"Officer Cooley," Cavanaugh began, as though saying his name aloud was a type of affirmation. Then he continued in a slow, apprehensive tone. "It's, uh, Cavanaugh. Cavanaugh Jones."

"Oh, Mr. Jones. I'm glad you called. We—"

"I've found something."

Cavanaugh cut the man off, his statement filling

the cabin of his car until he felt as if it would suffocate him. The silent line indicated the words might have also wrapped themselves around Cooley's throat as well.

CHAPTER TWELVE

The weeks continued to roll by and Sarah made great strides towards recovery, all except her memory, and Cavanaugh had managed to elude Cooley and his drone for a time. He had been so focused on Sarah and her recovery that he'd all but forgotten about what he'd found. The officers had shown up to retrieve the item, sending it to their lab to be processed. In a way, Cavanaugh felt relieved that he might, at last, get answers to the questions that had plagued him, ignoring the fear of what those answers might be. On the other hand, the implications of what would happen thereafter were uncertain and loomed like a shadow, following him everywhere.

Cavanaugh kept his focus on Sarah, whose doctors had cleared her for discharge, despite the fact that her mobility hadn't returned to normal. One thing, however, had returned, her vibrancy. Sarah's trademark spunk climbed out of hiding a bit more with every day, every stride, every small victory.

Henrietta pushed Sarah down the hall in a wheelchair one final time. Sarah had expressed mixed emotions about going home. She said she'd felt both excited and nervous. Cavanaugh's emotions were also at an imbalance, feeling more nervous than anything about Sarah returning to the estate since her assailant still roamed free, untouched.

"It has been quite the honor to care for you, Mrs. Sarah Jones." Henrietta blinked back tears but more filled her eyes anyway. She ran her middle finger along edge of her lower eyelid. "Watching you bounce back from your injuries with such vigor made me want to come to work everyday, just to see what you'd do next."

By now, Sarah's eyes were watering too.

"Don't tell the others, but you're my favorite." Henrietta smiled and Sarah giggled. "I'm sure going to miss you."

"I'm going to miss you too but I know where you work." Sarah winked.

Henrietta stooped down, cupped Sarah's face in her hand and gave another warm smile before flipping up the foot plates on her chair.

"Alright, time to get out of here!" Henrietta held a crutch out for Sarah, her consolation prize, since she still needed aid to walk.

Sarah hoisted herself up out of the chair and Cavanaugh jumped to her side to help.

"I've got it!" Sarah said, slapping his hands away. "Left up to you, you'd just carry me everywhere I needed to go. I'd never walk again!"

"Headstrong, that one, isn't she?" Henrietta said. It wasn't a question, more of an affirmation.

"And that's putting it lightly," Cavanaugh scoffed.

"I can hear you, ya know. I'm not hopped-up on painkillers anymore. You can't talk about me like I'm not here."

"Sorry, it's become habit to ignore you." Henrietta laughed, giving Sarah a light poke.

"If I didn't need my good leg to stand on, I'd use it to kick you."

In the midst of laughter Cavanaugh, Sarah and Henrietta traded hugs and goodbyes while loading Sarah and all her goodies into Cavanaugh's waiting car. Balloons, flowers and the like filled the back seat while Sarah occupied the front. It felt like ages since she'd sat in that seat. Once Cavanaugh got her home, they had an easy transition, settling back into life as they knew it, with a few exceptions.

Sarah behaved like an eight year old on Christmas morning. She writhed with anticipation as she sat up in bed, cramming forkfuls of the eggs Cavanaugh had cooked into her mouth. He had obtained, perhaps by osmosis, some slight culinary knowledge after her hospital stay. What he did in the kitchen wasn't enough to be considered a skill, but he almost qualified as a tolerable cook. By no means had Cavanaugh become good or comparable to a moderate cook, but the man could make a mean omelet. He'd made Sarah, what he called, a "deluxe" omelet breakfast, and though the savory dish may have been a good one, Sarah didn't take the time to taste it. She just needed to get it down. She would've skipped breakfast altogether if Cavanaugh hadn't insisted she eat. He had become a bit of a hardass, making certain she ate whether she wanted to or not and if he had to force-feed her, so be it. Sarah hadn't put up a fight this round because that would just lengthen the time she'd have to wait until they headed to the stables. She'd been cleared to ride again, and Cavanaugh thought she'd burst if she had to wait another week or day or, in this case, minute.

"I'm not doing CPR on you if you choke to death,"

Cavanaugh said, giving Sarah a sideways glance as he put a dish in the sink.

"It's okay," she responded around a mouthful of half masticated eggs. "I'll do it on myself if it'll get me to the stables quicker."

Cavanaugh laughed, but Sarah held a straight face. He shook his head, rolling his eyes, humored by her seriousness, which made it all a little funnier. He looked at her, half dressed, his eyes roving over her body, pausing in places scarred by the knife that had cut through her torso and legs. Cavanaugh marveled at how she'd healed—and not just her body but her also her spirit. Most of her bruises had disappeared and now she needed to regain the weight she'd lost.

Sarah had already donned her pants, riding chaps, and boots but her top half was covered by nothing but a pink, lacy bra. Cavanaugh thought, more wished, he'd have to wrestle her down to get her to eat this morning but to his dismay he didn't have to. She took the meal he'd made for her without a fight, although he would have welcomed a wrestling match where he could remove that bra with his teeth, among other things. Too much beside herself with excitement, however, Sarah had been anxious to get to the stables and the horses. She, clearly, couldn't be bothered with much else, not Cavanaugh nor his thirst for her.

"Done!" Sarah yelled, raising both hands in the air

as though she had been taking part in an eating contest. She would've won.

Cavanaugh pulled on a shirt. As he buttoned it, he watched as Sarah almost knocked her empty plate onto the floor, trying to hop out of bed. She flitted around the apartment so fast that he half expected to see sparks coming from her heels.

"Slow down," he demanded.

"No, you hurry up," she answered, a flash of her going by. "Ready?"

"I guess I have to be, don't I?

"Yep! Let's go!" With the impatience of an eager toddler, she grabbed his hand and pulled him out the door.

Sarah made a mad dash for the stables. If Cavanaugh's legs weren't so long, he would've had to exert effort to keep up with his pint-sized wife. She bee-lined to Casey's stall, and Cavanaugh went to the other side of the barn to groom and tack another steed. Cavanaugh's horse, Whiskey, boasted the rich color of the fine, aged libation Cavanaugh enjoyed so much, but he had not had a drink since the day Sarah got hurt. He could not shake the guilt that he could've prevented the entire ordeal had he not been passed out from drunkenness. He wouldn't chance losing her again. As a result he'd become a little overzealous in his attentiveness.

"Morning, Henry," Cavanaugh said.

Henry, hunched over in a corner of one of the stalls, stood erect. He leaned on the large shovel he'd been using to clean the cube-shaped space.

"Hey, boss. Someone's excited today." Henry hitched his head in the direction Sarah had gone.

"Understatement of the century, my friend."

"She didn't come and chat with me like she usually does."

"Don't count it against her; she barely said good morning to me." Cavanaugh and Henry chuckled. "Where are my parents?"

"Uh, well, Mrs. J went into town and Mr. J is on a run to LaCoste."

"Ok, well we're taking Casey and Whiskey out for a ride. Big surprise, huh?"

"Enormous." Henry's sarcastic tone made Cavanaugh chuckle again.

After brushing and tacking Whiskey, Cavanaugh walked over to the other side of the barn to Casey's stall. The door, bearing the horse's name, stood open.

"Hey, darlin'. Ready to hit the trail?" He asked as he walked up, assuming Sarah and Casey were inside.

He peeked in, but the stall was empty. No way she'd left without him.

"Sarah?" he called out, peering behind him to see where she might be. "Maybe she went to the wash bay. C'mon boy."

Cavanaugh moved forward, his gait languid and casual, giving Whiskey a few pats on the neck. He took the horse in a wide circle to turn him around. As he did, he saw something out of place. On the floor of the empty stall, amid a mound of hay, lay Casey's bridle. He squinted at it to make sure his eyes weren't deceiving him. When satisfied with what he knew it to be, he checked the hooks for the horse's halter. He found it, hanging right where it belonged. The stalls on either side were empty as were their designated hooks. This raised concern in Cavanaugh. In order to lead the horse, you needed a halter; to ride him, you needed a bridle with reins. All of the things that belonged to Casey, the things Sarah needed to ride him were all in their assigned spaces. All except the horse, of course.

Where had she gone? And why would she leave her tacking supplies? The simplest answer: she wouldn't. These thoughts floated around in Cavanaugh's mind as he tried to remain calm. He could feel a slow, ascending panic beginning to rise like bile in his throat. It burned and stung. No matter how he tried to force the feeling, the emotion, the panic, down it sprang up again, taking its original form like a memory foam mattress.

"Sarah?"

Cavanaugh called her name but again she didn't answer. He stood there, looking around for a moment, peeking into the stall again, as if he could've missed her standing there. As if by magic she'd appear just because he wanted her to.

"Okay, boy, stay here," he whispered to Whiskey.

He often reserved his quiet, calm tone for the horses, a way to quell them when they were excitable, but this time he used the tone more for himself than the horse. Cavanaugh led Whiskey into one of the empty stalls, rolled the door on its rails to a close, and hooked the latch to lock it. Taking careful steps around both barns, he poked his head into every stall searching for Sarah, whether empty or occupied.

"Hey, Henry?"

Cavanaugh had made it back to where Henry had been. His tools and supplies sat in the middle of the walkway, abandoned. Now Henry wasn't where he'd left him either, not that it was out of the ordinary. Who knew where he had disappeared to, or what other task he'd left this one behind to tend. Cavanaugh didn't think much of Henry's absence, except that he couldn't ask him if Sarah had happened by. He walked to the rear of the barns, surveying the fields as far as he could see thinking it would be somewhat hard to hide a 1200-pound gelding. He saw no one. He then checked the arena and the training pens, still, no one.

"What the hell!" Cavanaugh said aloud, though no one had been around to hear his words apart from himself.

He made a sprint for the pool house, looking all around him as he crossed the lush green lawn. He banged the door open to the apartment, calling for Sarah as he walked through. The apartment was vacant. He felt a pang of relief and panic at the same time. Relieved that he hadn't walked into his wife's blood again, and panic because he hadn't found her there. Leaving his front door wide open, Cavanaugh dashed over to the main house. With every step his panic grew, and so did the dread.

"Where the fuck did she go?"

Cavanaugh, during his search for Sarah, realized that he hadn't crossed paths with Henry again either. It hadn't been weird for Henry not to be where Cavanaugh had left him, but not running into him anywhere else on the property was quite out of the ordinary. Henry sometimes seemed omnipresent with the way he made his rounds on the estate.

"Sarah! Henry!"

Cavanaugh called for both of them as he crashed

into the main house. He yelled their names, checking every room, but neither answered nor appeared. Cavanaugh ran back to the apartment, intending to double check, in case he and Sarah had missed one another. Halfway there, he slowed to a stop, ending up at the rear of his car. Cavanaugh placed his hands on his knees, taking a few seconds to catch his breath.

As he crouched there, in a sliver of space where the pavement ended and the grass began, Cavanaugh saw a glimmer of gold. He leaned down further, breathing slower when he reached for shimmering gold. He pinched the object between his sizable fingers, and with a gentle tug, he pulled a fragile gold chain from the crevice. Careful not to destroy the delicate piece of jewelry, he flicked off some of the dirt embedded into its links. As he held it up to the sunlight, he followed the little horse charm with his eyes as it swayed side to side. The trinket twinkled with each sway, almost hypnotizing Cavanaugh when he'd stared at it, recognizing the necklace as the one Sarah had lost.

"Well, I'll be damned," he mumbled, wondering how the necklace had gotten there and how the cops had missed it. "Incompetent bastards."

Fueled by his resentment against the 'authorities,' Cavanaugh shoved the precious little necklace into his pocket and made the last few strides to their apartment. He ran through it again and rechecked the rooms, hoping for Sarah. Hoping for anything but the emptiness of not finding her, but that's what he ended up with, emptiness. Sarah wasn't there.

Cavanaugh didn't know what to do, what to think. Maybe she took another horse. Maybe she was searching for him and they were missing each other by mere seconds. Maybe. Cavanaugh knew these maybes were improbable and if they were possible, it wouldn't begin to explain the fact that Henry had disappeared too.

Cavanaugh decided to return to the barn for a once over, but before he did, he went back inside and grabbed his cell phone and his fifty caliber pistol. He had not kept a gun in the house since Sarah had first moved in because they freaked her out but, bit by bit, Cavanaugh had abolished her fear of guns, introducing parts of them like puzzle pieces. Small parts of a bigger picture. Then he taught her where the pieces fit, how to assemble a gun, the purpose of each element and then, the gun as a whole. Once past that, they progressed to target practice and she'd gotten quite good. Since then, Cavanaugh had kept at least one gun in the house as a measure of precaution.

Back at the barn, Cavanaugh still saw no signs of Henry or Sarah. Pulling out his cell phone, he dialed Henry's number. Soon after the call connected, he heard a singsong melody close by. Wheeling around, he looked for Henry, for his phone, walking in one direction and then the next until the ringing stopped. He disconnected the call and dialed his number again. Turning in wild circles,

Cavanaugh searched for the phone's location, knowing, by now, that Henry wasn't with it. He took tentative steps, following the song until he found Henry's phone in a wheelbarrow full of horse feed. The same barrow Henry had been scooping from when Cavanaugh left to meet Sarah on the other side of the barn. There Henry's phone lay, mocking him among the chunky bits.

"Shit!" He picked it up and saw his name on the phone's screen and slammed it back into the container of kibble.

Cavanaugh struggled to keep a leveled head, but the fear of Sarah being in danger or hurt again felt tangible to him. It burned in his throat, heated his hands, quaked his body. He ran to the other side of the barn and pulled the door open to the stall where he'd put Whiskey. He led the horse out, mounted him in a single leap, and headed towards the wooded trail. Cavanaugh gave Whiskey hard kicks to the flanks, making him race through the field, slowing once they reached the entry point to the woods. The trees soared high above like city skyscrapers. The leaves formed a canopy of shade, blocking out the sun and the leaves carried breezes on their small, fragile chariots, making the wind almost visible.

Cavanaugh wanted to rush along the worn path, excel his pace to make his search feel more avid, but he knew that wouldn't be productive. He knew that a slow, quiet search would be more effective, more thorough. He needed to be able to listen for Sarah and maybe Henry too. This awful, wretched déjà vu blanketed him like a cape of needles making him writhe and twitch. Cavanaugh tried, with little success, to quell the sickening feeling in his stomach as he called out for Sarah and Henry. His answer was the sound of the river.

"Sarah!" he yelled.

This time the river didn't answer, the forest floor did. Cavanaugh heard the snap of a twig and the crunch of dried leaves behind him. He whipped around, yanking at the reins to circle Whiskey, but he didn't see anything. He remained quiet, listening, his eyes darting around for evidence of movement other than his own. Another noise or something, undetected by Cavanaugh, made Whiskey's ears perk. The horse angled his ears toward the sound. Cavanaugh noticed Whiskey's reaction and followed an imaginary line with his eyes, but still, he didn't see or hear anything.

"Sarah, baby? Henry?"

Trepidation began to seep into or out of Cavanaugh's pores, hard to tell which. The scene felt much too reminiscent of what they'd lived out just a few months ago. Being in the woods, searching for Sarah again brought back flashes of the last time he'd found her. He saw blood and bruises, the pain in her face. He could taste it all in his mouth, smell it in his nostrils. Now, it didn't feel like months ago that she'd had to fight for her life but like days. Cavanaugh prayed for a different, a better outcome. Prayed that he'd find her healthy. Prayed that she'd jump out from behind a bush and yell 'Olly olly oxen free!' as if they'd been playing a wicked game of hide and seek.

He turned around again, searching as each minute stretched on, feeling indefinite. Amid the quiet, Cavanaugh's mind ran rampant with morbid possibilities, one of which included Henry as Sarah's assailant. He hadn't thought of it before. Had never given thought of the possibility that Henry could have hurt Sarah, after all, he had access...to everything. Cavanaugh hadn't thought about how convenient it would've been for him to do as he willed and clean up after himself. He couldn't imagine what motive Henry would have to do such a thing to Sarah but who would have one? Cavanaugh felt himself flush as he thought of how he'd given Henry the opportunity to get to Sarah by turning his back and leaving her alone but despite that, he called for Henry anyway.

"Sarah...Henry!"

"Boss?" Henry answered out of nowhere.

Startled, Cavanaugh drew his gun as if he were in a western gunfight. He had his fingers wrapped around the gun's handle, his grip so tight that it almost hurt. His index finger slid around the trigger and his thumb clicked off the safety.

"Henry?"

Cavanaugh scanned the area. Through a thicket of trees and brush, he spotted Henry astride one horse while leading another. Cavanaugh gave Whiskey a soft kick, walking them over. He hadn't put his gun away but had it aimed at the center of Henry's chest. He noticed that Henry had Casey trailing beside him and looked from Casey to Henry.

"What are you doing out here?" Cavanaugh asked, his hand tightening more around the grip of the gun.

Although Cavanaugh had a series of questions to ask, that one had been the first to make it to his lips despite having a more important question he needed an answer to.

"Where's Sarah, and why do you have Casey? She was tacking him to ride."

Cavanaugh didn't wait for answers, not certain that he'd wanted them. He peered at Henry, wary of him because of all the scenarios he'd conjured up. Then he realized something was wrong. So caught up in his own thoughts and worry, he hadn't noticed Henry panting and the beads of sweat dotting his forehead. The weather wasn't warm enough to induce sweat, and Henry had been walking the horses at a slow pace. He couldn't have been exerting enough energy to cause visible affects. Cavanaugh also noticed that Henry hadn't made a single sound since he'd spotted him, aside from calling him "boss".

Cavanaugh squinted, observing Henry closer but never lowering his gun. He noted how Henry held the reins and the lead in one hand and the way his body slumped close to Tebo's head. Cavanaugh knew the dangers of hovering so close to the horse's head and he also knew Henry to be well versed about those hazards as well. This fact prompted Cavanaugh to scrutinize the man more. He looked at Henry's eyes, they were wide and somewhat unfocused. Moving a little closer, Cavanaugh saw Henry's other arm hanging limp at his side. Something wasn't right. As Cavanaugh craned his neck to see, he held the gun steady, unwilling to let his guard down.

"Henry," Cavanaugh pulled himself upright. "Where's Sarah?" He spoke in a calm, soft tone, a very conscious effort for him. Henry didn't respond. "Henry?"

Cavanaugh moved Whiskey about a foot closer to the dazed man and that's when he got a full view of Henry's arm. From elbow to fingertips, rivulets of blood made active, flowing streams down his arm. Curvy lines wrapped around his forearm, streaking his skin down to the fingers where the blood dripped to the ground. Cavanaugh lowered his gun, his arm falling little by little until it landed at his side. The shock registered on Cavanaugh's face as he viewed the large, v-shaped gash in the crook of his Henry's arm, the source of his bloody river. Cavanaugh, for a long minute, stared at the injured man, until Henry spoke.

"Mr. Jones," Henry said in a tone so low that it

didn't qualify as a whisper. "...Ms. Sarah." He managed to get Sarah's name out on a labored breath.

Henry threw his head to the side, signaling behind him. Cavanaugh looked beyond Henry, but saw nothing. Maybe Henry was confused or, perhaps, delirious, in shock.

"Henry, I'm right here."

Cavanaugh felt sorry for him and a bit guilty for his thoughts, but part of him still didn't trust him. He moved close to Henry's injured side and realized there'd been more to his injury than a slashed elbow. Henry held his arm close to his side and behind it, Cavanaugh saw the hilt of a knife. Henry's blood-soaked shirt covered the wound where he'd been stabbed in the side. A wound with the knife still in it.

"Fuck me!" Cavanaugh muttered. "Shit, Henry."

Cavanaugh tucked his gun into the waist of his pants behind his back and positioned Whiskey within inches of Tebo. He stifled the blazing bile at the back of his throat when he got closer to the gash. Endless streams of blood, the soft flesh, never meant to be seen, lay open for his craven eyes. Leaning over the other side of his horse, Cavanaugh heaved. He turned back to Henry, thinking he'd emptied himself out, but then he threw up again, the act more violent than the time before.

"Okay," Cavanaugh said to himself.

Henry, being a slight man, much smaller than Cavanaugh, made it easy to produce a sort of tourniquet for Henry. Cavanaugh removed his belt, and after a hard swallow, he took hold of Henry's arm. Looping his belt around the man's torso, Cavanaugh bent Henry's arm upwards, hoping it would hamper the bleeding. He secured his arm in place by buckling the belt around it, grimacing as Henry groaned in pain.

"Sorry, buddy."

Cavanaugh wiped his hands on his jeans and took Casey's lead from Henry's relentless clutch. He noticed, for the first time, that Casey had been lassoed.

"I'll call for help. Is Sarah back there?" Cavanaugh gestured in the direction Henry had come from.

Henry gave a vague nod. Regardless of Cavanaugh's conflicting thoughts, he felt obligated not to let the man bleed to death, at least not until he found out what he did... or knew. Cavanaugh gave Tebo a heavy slap on the flank and watched as they broke through the trees towards the field. Henry bobbed on Tebo's back, and though unsteady, he managed to stay on. Cavanaugh hopped down and tied Casey to a nearby tree, before he and Whiskey headed deeper into the woods. He continued searching for Sarah, praying to find her in better condition than he'd found Henry.

"God, if you're there, please...Please let her be okay."

Galloping along the trail, Cavanaugh thought he may be moving too fast to listen for Sarah but he couldn't help himself. Then he remembered he needed to call an ambulance for Henry. After slowing down, Cavanaugh pulled his phone from his pocket and dialed 911, hoping he'd just need one emergency vehicle. Within seconds, an operator came on the line.

"I need an ambulance. Someone's been stabbed," Cavanaugh spoke in a rush, and never gave the operator a chance to ask questions, rattling off his address before hanging up.

Just as he put his phone into his shirt pocket, Cavanaugh felt a sharp pain in his left shoulder. It struck him with a force that propelled him backwards, spooking Whiskey. The horse responded by rising up on his hind legs, neighing while throwing Cavanaugh from his back. He landed on a patch of hardened dirt, the impact taking the air from his lungs. The pain in Cavanaugh's shoulder intensified, feeling like a bolt of lightning had been shot through his collarbone and out of his shoulder blade. Amid a wheeze, he yelped out in pain, his voice sounding like someone else's. He rolled over onto his side and squeezed his eyes shut with such force he saw flashing circles of blue and white light. As if a colored disco ball were spinning round and round behind his eyelids. Cavanaugh thought he might have been having a heart attack.

Writhing on the ground, he rolled onto his other side, stifling a scream, the pain intense enough to cause his eyes to fly open. He felt as if he were hallucinating, seeing something protruding from his chest. He used his right arm to reach for it.

"Ahhh!" he yelled out in pain, but touching the object had been enough to convince him that he wasn't imagining things, as if the pain hadn't been enough.

Cavanaugh had been shot with a spiked, carbon, hunting arrow. It had plunged through the front of his body, the sharp, pointed arrow ripping through his flesh. The thunderous pain felt so intense, it roared in his head at a deafening volume.

His eyes roved in a wild search as he surveyed the immediate area. Whiskey had run off and although he couldn't see it, he could hear the river. Laying on his back, Cavanaugh shifted his position enough to angle his head so he could look toward the sound of the rushing water. He knew a deer stand was located on the other side of it, one he'd used many times, but never like this. Never hunting man, only beast. In an unexpected turn of events, Cavanaugh had become the hunted, prompting compassion for the animals he'd shot and killed.

Before Cavanaugh could set his gaze on the river, he spotted something more unsettling than being prey for a hunter. In a cruel twist of convoluted irony, Cavanaugh lay just a few yards from the boulder where he'd first found Sarah black-eyed and bleeding. This had to be some sick form of reciprocity for all the emotional distress he'd caused every woman he'd ever dated—all but the one he had married, but still she hadn't been immune to his deplorable behaviors. He regretted it all now.

Cavanaugh had found Sarah again. Just as before, he couldn't see all of her, her body visible from the waist down and near the same place he'd found her before. Would her condition be the same as well? She wasn't moving. She didn't make the clicking sound at the back of her throat. She lay motionless. No, this would not be like the last time; she was not in the same condition. This time might be worse than the last.

Cavanaugh, as much as he wanted to, couldn't bear to call her name, afraid of the quiet that would follow. His eyes stung and he squeezed them shut against the building heat. When he opened them, he looked at Sarah again, pulling and dragging himself across the ground toward her body. Then he heard a rustling beyond him. Cavanaugh stopped moving, looking in every direction he could. He wanted to sit up to get a better view, but didn't want to make himself more visible or accessible. When the woods went quiet again, except for the river, he continued to claw his way over to Sarah. It felt like a mile from where he'd started to where she lay.

"Seej? Baby?" He reached out and stroked her temple.

He positioned his body to frame her head, shielding her from exposure. He leaned down and pressed his cheek to hers, begging her to wake up with quiet murmurs.

"Baby, wake up. Please, please, please, wake up," he pled into her ear, but she didn't answer.

Cavanaugh's hope began to crumble until he felt a soft heat on his neck. The bursts of heat came in well-timed increments. It took Cavanaugh a measure of time to conclude that the puffs of heat were Sarah's breath. Excited, he pulled himself up much too fast, sending a wave of pain through the left side of his body. He grunted, welcoming the physical pain over the pain he'd felt in the wake of almost losing her for the second time. He stared at her, motionless, a look of astonishment on his face.

"There must be a God," he said. "Babe, can you hear me?" He shook her with his functional arm.

A twig snapped close by and Cavanaugh leaned in closer to Sarah as he looked to see where the noise had come from. He imagined the hunter spying his prey, hoping to score two for the price of one. Cavanaugh had almost forgotten about the gun he'd tucked away, realizing he couldn't feel the cold steel against his skin anymore. Dammit! he thought. It must have fallen out when Whiskey had thrown him.

Surveying the space around them, Cavanaugh saw a fawn, taking an easy walk toward the river's edge. Upon spotting him, the fawn went the other way, disappearing into the brush. He breathed a sigh of relief and turned his attention back to Sarah. He kept whispering for her to waken as though his will alone would be enough to do so. He didn't know where her injuries were nor did he see any blood, and he assumed that to be a good sign.

"Sarah, please baby."

At that moment, Sarah's eyes began to flutter, enough reason to induce near unbridled excitement in Cavanaugh. He kept calling out to her, getting more of a reaction each time. Just beyond the sound of his voice, he heard a faint melody somewhere in the distance. He thought he'd imagined it but the tune had a hint of familiarity, though he couldn't pinpoint it. The tune and the direction from which it came were both lost upon him. Cavanaugh felt a strange emotion lick the surface of his skin, causing goose flesh to rise and the prickled hairs on his body to stand at attention. The melody moved closer, got louder, creating an intensified sense of urgency.

"Come on, baby, you've got to wake up," Cavanaugh still spoke in soothing tones but when those murmurs proved ineffective he lost it. "Sarah Elaine Jones! Wake! The fuck! Up!"

Cavanaugh assigned every word its own zip code

and gave Sarah as hard a shake as he could manage. If she could hear him at all, she'd respond to that. One of the things Cavanaugh loved most about Sarah was that she didn't take his shit...at least not all of it. She had an answer, a comeback, a witty or equally bitter retaliation for everything.

Just as Cavanaugh expected she would, Sarah responded to his outburst, peeling her eyes halfway open and closing them again. Sarah tried to open her eyes, having more success the second time around. She kept trying, blinking her eyes in rapid succession as though using the Morse code to communicate with him. Meanwhile, the tune he'd heard continued to come closer to them. The sharp, whistling tune bounced and echoed off the trees that surrounded them. Consternated, Cavanaugh furrowed his brow, wondering where he'd heard the tune. His mind traced a maze of hidden clues as he worked to discern the tune, the whistle, and then a light clicked on in his mind.

CHAPTER THIRTEEN

"Cav?" Sarah spoke, her voice faint, lifting her hand to touch his face.

She gasped when her eyes settled on the arrow protruding from his chest. To Sarah, it looked like a prop, like something you'd see in a store of practical jokes or Halloween garb. Except it wasn't. The very real arrow had pierced her husband and it was no practical joke. Sarah couldn't figure how Cavanaugh could breathe, for her breath had caught on the sight alone.

"Cav, oh my god!" Cavanaugh turned to face Sarah. Her hands hovered over him, falling in light pats as though he were a fragile Faberge egg. "You've been shot," she said, as if he'd needed reminding.

"Yeah," Cavanaugh said, his tone dismissive. "Are

you hurt? What happened?"

"We've got to get out of here." Sarah's eyes darted around.

"Sarah!" he reached for her. "Are you hurt?"

"I'm fine, Cav. I just have a bump on the head, but you're bleeding. We have to get you some help and get away from here before he comes back. Can you walk?"

She had sat up, kneeling next to Cavanaugh, inspecting his body, hoping he could walk, but needing him to be able to run. Cavanaugh didn't have the chance to respond, he had not lifted up onto his elbow before both Sarah's attention shifted towards a familiar sound. In unison, Sarah and Cavanaugh's heads whipped in the direction of a whistling tune, accompanied by footfalls. Each step sounded louder as nature's dried, crackled floor crunched beneath approaching feet. While Cavanaugh sighed with relief, collapsing back to the ground, Sarah went rigid with anxiety and fear.

"Baby, we've gotta go. Now! Come on." Sarah shuffled sideways, but Cavanaugh didn't move. "Cav! Come on!"

Sarah's eyes filled with fear as she looked around, anticipating the moment they'd be spotted. She pulled on Cavanaugh's arm as he lay there, relaxed, showing no signs of panic or urgency. A shadow appeared, stretching across the ground in their direction.

"Babe, it's just—" Cavanaugh began, turning to Sarah, but she'd vanished. He looked left, then right, sitting up and falling against the rock with a hard thump.

"Son of a bitch!" he exclaimed, and she'd left no evidence of which way she'd gone. "Sarah!"

He saw no sign of her and just as he inhaled to call out to her again, the whistling stopped. So did the encroaching footsteps. Cavanaugh faced forward, his eyes making a trail upward from where the shadow touched him to look at the figure standing over him.

"Thank God," Cavanaugh released a sigh. "Dad, can you help me find Sarah? She was just here and I don't know where she ran off to."

Artemis stood still, staring down at his son, but didn't say a word.

"Dad, did you hear me?" he paused. "Dad!"

Cavanaugh swore, about to follow the one profanity with a string of others until he observed a handful of abnormalities in his father's presence. Art usually kept his hair neat but his wispy grays flew in various directions, looking uncombed and disheveled. Cavanaugh noted the haggard look of his face, a great departure from his normal fresh-faced look. His pupils were dilated, so much so that his irises were but slivered rings. Cavanaugh noticed something else, a small thing, but no less strange. Looking up at his father, he watched as Art gnawed on a piece of chewing gum. Artemis never chewed gum; in fact, he hated gum. He hated when other people chewed gum.

The more Cavanaugh noticed, the more confused he became. He let his eyes roam, scrutinizing one oddity after another: Art's stance, his posture, his attire. All different from his normal, every day character. He stood with his weight shifted to one side, when he would most always stand square. He slouched, his shoulders hunched forward, and he wore shorts and a polo. Cavanaugh had never known his father to own any such clothing, let alone wear them. The man looked as if he were on his way to the golf course, not the woods. Art didn't golf and his wardrobe consisted of flannel and jeans, not polos and khakis. Cavanaugh scrutinized him, not sure whether to be wary or worry. He opened his mouth to speak again but closed it when Art pulled out his bow.

It seemed to materialize, whether out of the air, or a nearby tree, or from the ground, Cavanaugh couldn't decide. Just as the bow had appeared, so did an arrow. An arrow identical to the one still running through

Cavanaugh's flesh. He hadn't moved, leaning on the same rock where Sarah had been, watching as Art positioned the nock of the arrow to the bowstring, his movements adroit. In slow motion, Art, holding the arrow in place, pulled his arm back. He aligned his hand with his cheek, grazing his face as he drew the arrow toward him until the string stretched taut and rigid.

"Dad, what are you doing?" Art didn't answer.

Cavanaugh looked around, no sign of anything to hunt, no one but him. Cavanaugh slid sideways as panic began to rise within him.

"Dad!"

Cavanaugh slid back another inch. Using his uninjured arm, he tried to leverage himself against the rock so he could stand but his attempt failed. He slipped, scrapping the heel of his hand against the rock as he fell back to the ground.

"Ugh!" he wailed, squeezing his eyes shut against the pain.

Artemis dawdled as if to taunt Cavanaugh, never speaking a word, just watching as he pushed back one inch at a time. Outrunning the arrow Art had loaded would be impossible, supposing Cavanaugh wasn't hurt. Each measured pull added an increased degree of speed. Cavanaugh sat in a shocked state of silence, staring at the tip of the sharp, pointed, broad-head arrow Art aimed at him, paralyzed, not by fear but, by disbelief.

"Dad, what are you doing? What the fuck are you doing?"

Cavanaugh couldn't discern if Art's intended target was his heart or the space between his eyes. It didn't matter much, because both meant absolute death. Cavanaugh had, at least, a thousand thoughts within the few seconds that ticked by, Sarah being among the first. He felt grateful, joyous, that she'd run off, leaving him to die alone and out of her sight. The other thoughts were a flood of flashbacks, findings, and disenchantments. Guilty fingers all pointed to Artemis Jones, despite Cavanaugh's previous unwillingness to believe.

After Sarah's surgery, the doctors told Cavanaugh that they'd pulled a tiny piece of the knife she'd been stabbed with from her side. No one thought it unusual considering the circumstances surrounding her injuries, until the authorities found a broken knife among his father's collection. They'd also found a torn and crumpled picture of Sarah. Regardless of the finger covering part of the lens, Sarah, bloodied and standing amid the woods, had still been identifiable. The cops had speculated about the identity of the photographer, but had no leads on who'd taken the photo.

Cavanaugh had found, in his car, a pair of bent,

misshapen glasses, a blood stained fingerprint on the lens. He had irrefutable evidence staring him in the face. He'd also taken notice of the knife in Henry's side, another one that belonged in his father's vast collection. Cavanaugh had not rationalized any of these facts before, but wished he had long before this unthinkable scene had unfolded.

Cavanaugh, confident that the cops would arrive in enough time to save his wife, would have to be the sacrificial lamb, the collateral damage against Sarah's life. His mouth went dry as he realized that this may very well be his last moments, not that talking or yelling at Art had done him any good. The man still had not spoken, hovering over Cavanaugh with his weapon aimed square at him.

While Cavanaugh stared at him, he still couldn't believe the man in front of him was his father. He couldn't be the man who took up for him when Cynthia berated him with insults and put downs. He couldn't fathom this to be the same man who'd loved and doted on Sarah like an infant child. Or the man who'd encouraged him when he'd pitched asinine ideas doomed to fail. He couldn't be the man who'd stood beside him when he stepped in line and stepped out of it. He couldn't be the same man who towered over him, a hunter of men, poised to kill: his son, his employee, his daughter-in-law. Although staring into the face of truth, Cavanaugh had trouble believing.

The sun flashed through the trees for a split second,

blinding Cavanaugh. He squinted against it, closing his eyes to shield the brightness.

Better not to see it coming anyway, he thought.

POW! The unmistakable crackle of gunfire pierced the air. Cavanaugh fell to the ground, searing pain burned his flesh. He felt the warmth of blood on his skin. The deafening ring of the shot amid the quiet woods produced a lingering shrill that muffled the sounds of nature: the river, the scurry of wildlife, the rustling of the leaves in the wind. Cavanaugh lay beside the rock, in stillness, in darkness. The arrow Art aimed at Cavanaugh had struck, streaking through the air seconds after the gun went off.

The longest moment trickled by before Cavanaugh peeled his eyes open. Through his ringing ears, he'd heard the whiz of Art's arrow followed by the thud of something falling to the ground. However, the most haunting sound had to be the uncontrollable, anguished cry from Sarah. Cavanaugh made slow, deliberate half-circles with his eyes as he opened them. When he looked up, he saw the sun peeking through the canopy of leaves, just to hide again behind them. Looking left, then right, he saw that he was still in the woods, still laying near the boulder, and when he looked down he saw just one arrow going through him. The other arrow lay beside him, having sliced his ear, explaining the burning pain he felt there. He gave himself a once over. He wasn't dead, he wasn't shot, although the same couldn't be said for the body next to him. Artemis, his father, lay lifeless, facedown among the fallen leaves and branches.

Cavanaugh, at last, raised his eyes and pushed himself up on his elbow. He looked at Sarah. She sat on the ground with her knees drawn up to her chest, but spread far enough apart to hold his gun between them. Her hands were steady as she held the weapon, still aimed where Art had stood, wisps of smoke spiraling from the gun's barrel. Her body shook with the convulsions of her sobs but her hands were steadfast, as were her eyes for she never took her gaze from the target, just as Cavanaugh had taught her.

Incredulity lined Cavanaugh's face, awed by his wife and her courage. She'd saved his life with one shot. If she'd aimed anywhere below Art's neck, the situation may have become a double tragedy. The flash Cavanaugh assumed to be sunlight turned out to be the glistening metal of the gun.

"Seej," Cavanaugh spoke just above a whisper.

She reacted fast, swinging her tensed arms around to point the gun at him. Her chest heaved, erratic with breath but, although her eyes were trained in Cavanaugh's direction, she didn't seem to see him. He didn't move, fearing Sarah would react again by pulling the trigger.

In the distance, Cavanaugh saw a clandestine team of swat members, peppered among the trees and bushes. Without moving too much or too fast, he signaled for them to hold their positions, bringing his eyes right back to Sarah. He held his stare in place until she looked at him, remaining as still as possible. A long minute passed and then another before Sarah looked into Cavanaugh's eyes. He knew she would, he knew all it would take was a look. That's all it ever took. He watched her eyes as they found his, and her sobs intensified, something he didn't think possible.

Cavanaugh gave a small nod and Sarah let the gun fall to the ground between her feet. She covered her face with her hands and continued to sob. By the time she removed her hands the area had filled with officers, detectives, and swat team members. Cavanaugh kept his eyes locked on her and neither moved. His head swam like the river fish, making him feel drunk. He managed to give Sarah a wink and then tipped his imaginary hat to her, same as he'd done the day they'd met. A tiny grin formed at one corner of Sarah's mouth, the last image Cavanaugh would see, his final memory.

CHAPTER FOURTEEN

Sarah walked the halls of St. Luke's as if visiting a friend's house. She spoke to one person and then another as she made her way down the corridor. Her face revealed her worry and grief but her attitude did not when she talked with Henrietta. She and the playful nurse kept a running tab of banter, Henrietta giving her shit as always.

St. Luke's buzzed with familiar sounds. Beeping and whirring machines. The quiet shuffle of rubber-soled shoes on the smooth linoleum floor. The soft sound of breathing, rhythmic and measured. Hushed voices bounced back and forth, the quiet words evaporating before they reached ears not meant to hear the conversation.

"How's it going, Mrs. Jones?" Henrietta walked in, her smile wide.

"I so love the sound of that!" Sarah responded.

"I know, that's why I said it."

As the two women continued their own conversation, a slow state of consciousness, awareness, crept over Cavanaugh. He couldn't quite make out the words they spoke, so he listened to the other sounds around him. His heartbeat increased with the thoughts that began to crowd his mind. St. Luke's Hospital had become familiar territory. Cavanaugh's panic began to rise, climbing with his formidable emotions bubbling to the surface.

Oh my God, Cavanaugh thought, lamenting to the invisible being most of the people he knew prayed to. Not again! No, not again! God, please, you could not possibly be this cruel! Please, if you do exist and I think you do, please don't let Sarah suffer like this again. You saved her the first time; you heard me and saved her. I know I'm asking a lot, probably too much considering we've never met, but if I have to trade my life for hers...I will. Just...

Click, click, click, click.

Cavanaugh heard yet another familiar sound, one he knew well, followed by a heavy sigh. His heart raced so fast, it became painful as he fought against the fog to hear, to see something, to feel...anything. Anything but grief. Cavanaugh's body reacted to his thoughts, his panic becoming tangible. His fear transformed into a force he could feel. It spiraled around him, the effects evident in his hands and arms, then his shoulders. His legs were the last to feel the effect. He couldn't decipher how long he'd been caught in the vortex, but he did notice when the calm descended. Falling upon him like a warm blanket, soothing and soft.

Another measure of time passed that he couldn't discern. His eyelids felt less heavy, a little less like they'd been glued shut, and he willed them to open. He needed to make sure Sarah was okay. He needed to see her with his own eyes. Cavanaugh heard a pen scribbling on paper, then the paper crumpling. It sounded loud among the quiet. The soft clicking started again, drawing him further into awareness. When he pulled his eyes open after a few tries, the haze dissipated, slinking away like a fog, making a way for cognizance.

He expected to see Sarah, once again laid in a hospital bed, battered and bruised. He tried to prepare himself for an image that resembled her, knowing the road to reclaiming her original self would be a hard one. He resolved to stand by her, cheer her on, encourage her, help her heal. With a heavy breath Cavanaugh tried to focus his gaze, summon his strength. A dry erase board hung on the wall in his direct line of sight, he read the sloppy scribble written on its surface, indicating the patient's pertinent information: Jones, Cavanaugh; Allergies: penicillin, blueberries. Cavanaugh felt a slight furrow at his brow. He couldn't understand why his name and allergy information had been written on the board? Had God heard him and spared his Sarah? Cavanaugh's gaze trailed downward to the foot of the bed. A blanket covered his big feet and he willed his right foot to move, just to make sure it belonged to him. It did. Little by little, he observed the body in the bed, his body: the ugly hospital gown, the tubes going in and out everywhere, the rise and fall of his chest.

Cavanaugh looked toward the sound of the clicking and the rumpling paper. In a chair, next to his hospital bed, sat Sarah. God had heard him, had listened when he'd asked to trade places. He's the one who lay helpless in a bed, not she. The machines monitored his heartbeat and vital signs while she sat in comfort without wires, or tubes or an ugly gown. Sarah looked perfect, unharmed, a newspaper in front of her face, once again filling in the blanks of the crossword puzzle.

Sarah didn't see Cavanaugh staring at her, didn't seem aware of the nervous clicks she made in the back of her throat. Cavanaugh couldn't remember Sarah ever looking so beautiful, in spite of only being able to see her forehead. A wave of relief washed over him, making his head swim. He smiled but kept quiet for a minute or two longer while he stared at his wife. The woman who'd saved his life. Mrs. Jones.

"Ahem!" Cavanaugh feigned clearing his throat.

Sarah peered over the top of her newspaper, peeling back the corner until Cavanaugh could see one of her starburst eyes. In that split second eye contact with Cavanaugh, Sarah threw her paper to the ground and leapt into his arms.

An uninhibited, childlike giggle escaped Sarah as she thrust herself forward, grabbing hold of Cavanaugh's face, and planted damp miniature kisses all over it. Pockets of glee laced the space in between breath and sound, as if she were a six-year-old who'd just been told she'd get to go to Disney World. Her giggles drowned out his grunts of pain and he had squeezed his eyes tight enough to see floating spots. He felt pained and exhilarated all at once. Knowing, seeing and feeling Sarah's body, her healthy body all over him was worth the pain...almost. It was obvious Sarah hadn't given any thought to his injuries. She kissed his bandages as though they weren't there and crushed his sling-supported arm beneath her body.

"Sarah, honey?" Cavanaugh managed to push the words through clenched jaws as he nudged Sarah away from the side of him that hurt the most.

"Oh! Cav, I'm so sorry. I'm just so excited!"

"I can see that."

She pulled herself upright and stood beside him. Sarah bent over and planted another batch of kisses on his cheek and neck and then his lips.

"Are you okay?"

"I was, until you did a belly flop on top of me." A sly grin spread across his face and Sarah punched his uninjured arm.

"Ow! No sympathy for an injured man, geez!"

Cavanaugh had been in the hospital for a few days, having lost so much blood when the doctors had removed the piercing arrow he'd had to have a blood transfusion. In a way he'd never imagined, Sarah had saved his life, not once, but twice. Her universal blood type had allowed her to give her blood in order to save him.

"Where are my parents? Is my dad here too?" Cavanaugh asked.

Tears glistened in Sarah's eyes, streaking her face almost the same instant that they'd appeared. She shook her head, plopping so hard down into her chair it scraped backwards a few inches. She flinched at the loud noise. Sarah couldn't seem to find her words. Her mouth fell open, staying that way as if she needed to breathe through it. She continued to shake her head 'no', but before she could locate her voice, Henrietta walked in.

"Well, well, look who decided to wake up. Had nice nap there, 'Beauty'?"

Cavanaugh managed a smile. "How do we keep getting stuck with you?" he asked.

"Glutton for punishment." Henrietta let out a small giggle.

Sarah swiped away her tears with the back of her hand so fast, Cavanaugh wondered if he'd imagined them.

"I'll say!" Sarah added.

They continued their ribbing while Henrietta ran her routine system of checks and balances on Cavanaugh, but as soon as Henrietta stepped over the threshold, exiting the room, Sarah's tears reappeared as if on cue.

"Babe," Cavanaugh cooed. "Why are you crying?"

"Art..." Sarah took in a shaky breath. "Art's dead."

She choked on the last word, tears running rivulets down her cheeks. Her nose became red and her eyelids flushed. As Cavanaugh looked at her, he couldn't help but see beyond her snivels to her beauty. As for his father, he wasn't surprised to hear the news, but the acidity, the sting, still struck him with an unexpected jolt. Cavanaugh reflected for a moment, on the image of his father standing over him with a pulled bow, aimed at him in way that would have guaranteed his death. He remembered hearing the gunshot. It rang in his ears again, causing him to start. The jolt brought him back to the present, back to the realization that the single shot had killed his father.

"What about my mom? And Henry? Where are they?" Cavanaugh watched as Sarah tried to gather her wits, the effort looking tangible.

"They discharged Henry yesterday, and your mom's been arrested." Sarah's tone remained somber.

"Arrested! What for?"

Cavanaugh figured there would be an ill fate for his father but, although his mother's behavior had been strange, what had she to do with any of it? Why had she been arrested? Before Sarah had the chance to answer him, someone knocked on the door.

"Mr. and Mrs. Jones?" The door opened and a familiar voice streamed in through the crack.

"Yes," Sarah answered.

"Can we come in?"

"Sure."

Officers Cooley and Pine were once again standing in a hospital room with Cavanaugh and Sarah, no doubt with a bevy of questions to ask.

The officers were bound to come by at some point. They'd been stopping by to check on Cavanaugh while working their case. A case more twisted than anyone could have ever imagined. It was like being thrust in the middle of a crime show, similar to the ones on TLC and the Discovery channel.

"How are you feeling, Mr. Jones?" Pine asked. "We were worried about you for a minute there."

"Well, I'm not being hunted anymore, so I guess that's a good thing."

"Certainly," Pine said around a titter, his face revealing his ambivalence. Cooley shot him a reproving look and Pine mouthed his apology.

"Have you been informed about your family?" Cooley's expression almost looked regrettable.

"No," Cavanaugh lied. "What's happened to them?"

"Well, your father sustained a gunshot wound to the back of the neck, severing the carotid artery. He died in transit to the hospital." Cooley paused, waiting a moment before continuing. When Cavanaugh didn't respond, Cooley spoke again. "Your mother has been arrested for aiding and abetting. She had knowledge of the crimes your father had committed."

"Crimes?" Cavanaugh put heavy emphasis on the plural word. "What do you mean, crimes?"

Cavanaugh eyed Cooley as the officer turned his gaze to Sarah, giving her a cursory glance. Cavanaugh's eyes then shifted to his wife who stared at the floor.

"What the hell is going on?" Cavanaugh asked,

certain they knew something he didn't.

"Well, this isn't the first time Artemis has attacked someone, apparently. Your mother, Cynthia, kept a detailed journal. We found it when we searched your estate. It had times, dates and information about every violent act Artemis had committed over the years. She'd also helped him by destroying evidence. Let me rephrase that,—"

"What the hell do you mean, 'this isn't the first time'?" Cavanaugh cut him off. "My father—"

"Mr. Jones," Pine interrupted. "We have reason to believe your father had a mental illness. We've found evidence indicating that he'd been diagnosed with Dissociative Identity Disorder." Cavanaugh scrunched his brows, his confusion evident in his face. Pine continued. "It's commonly referred to as multiple personality disorder."

Pine went on to explain the notes he'd found in Cynthia's diary. They'd discovered the diary hidden in a pocket of space behind a loose tile under the vanity of his parents' master bathroom. It chronicled the injuries, deaths, and destruction of evidence concerning multiple women over a period of thirty years. They had also found a file, which contained copies of medical documents, including Art's diagnosis and prescriptions—which Cynthia slipped into his coffee every morning. Art had an extreme aversion to medication, often refusing to take aspirin for a headache.

According to the records, Art had spent a considerable amount of time in the hospital under an assumed name and also as another personality with Cynthia by his side, which explained why he had no recollection of the events. It turned out to be the reason she couldn't stand to be in or around hospitals. Art, oblivious to his condition or the others that resided in his psyche, had no knowledge of his transition from one to the other, just blocks of time where he couldn't remember anything, which he'd contributed to his old age.

Cynthia, had kept a watchful eye on Art, having become aware of his transitions and the traits and characteristics of at least four of his varied personalities. The morning of Sarah's attack Cynthia had slept in. It wasn't something she ever did and by the standards of others, it may not have been considered sleeping in, at all. However, it was later than normal for her. When she'd awakened, Art had already left for Brady—so she thought. This meant that she hadn't made his coffee, which also meant he had not had his medication for the day. Most times, if Art went a morning, perhaps two, without his meds, he managed pretty well. It took a while for the fog of the medication to clear enough to wake the others. However, Art had just returned from a two-day trip and had another trip scheduled for that morning. It seemed of no consequence since Cynthia always woke before he did, without fail...aside for that morning.

Cynthia had been in the stables for a few minutes when Sarah showed up, bouncing with her usual excitement. The two exchanged a few cordial words and performed their separate duties. Cynthia went to the other barn where they kept most of their training equipment to retrieve some needed items, but when she returned, Casey and Sarah were gone. She hadn't been gone long and assumed Sarah had gone riding. She'd seen Sarah groom and tack Casey beforehand, so she had no reason to suspect anything different. A while later, when Cavanaugh came running to her in a panic, she'd thought he was just overreacting since he had such a flair for the dramatic.

For years, Cynthia had been covering for Art, burning incriminating evidence against him, keeping her in a constant tizzy, performing a never-ending list of chores, and ensuring the "order" of everything. This frenzied state of being had been her coverall, her way of keeping a handle on Art and his indiscretions. She did it all to keep her family intact, their name unmarred and anyone from ever finding out the truth. The journals were her one outlet, and she'd never told a soul, had never said it aloud. Cynthia endured the weight of the secret she held, not able to talk about it with her husband. As a result, she'd become cold and wary of anyone who lingered too long around her family. She didn't allow herself the comfort of being vulnerable with anyone, afraid she'd spill their well-guarded secret just to relieve the pressure. Cynthia couldn't take the risk. The exposure wasn't worth it. Besides, she had never told her own son who deserved to know. For all she had done, that was the one thing she didn't have the heart to do.

"All of this is written in her journals. Detailed accounts of every incident. She said she didn't have the heart to tell you," Pine looked at Cavanaugh with sympathetic eyes.

"Of course," Cooley chimed in. "Now she doesn't have to."

It was Pine's turn to give Cooley admonishing look.

⁂

Cavanaugh and Sarah both sat with their mouths agape, disbelief shading their eyes like dark makeup. Sarah had a hard time taking in what she'd heard. She couldn't imagine how Cavanaugh felt, if she was having a hard time. She could not believe, fathom, or picture any of what the officers had told them about their findings about Art, about Cynthia, about these people who'd become her family. She wondered what went through Cavanaugh's mind, his heart. Hers ached over the loss of Art and, in a weird way, sympathized with Cynthia and the weight of what she'd been carrying for the sake of her family. Despite the onerousness of everything the officers had revealed, it wickedly put things in perspective, helping Sarah to somewhat understand Art and Cynthia's actions, although dispelling them or forgiving them was a different matter.

Somehow, Sarah found her voice and while Cavanaugh still appeared speechless, she asked, "So what happens now?"

"Well, first we have to—" Cooley spoke, but almost as soon as he did, Sarah's mind wandered, despite her interest in his answer.

She felt awful for Cynthia and worse for thinking ill of her before. She couldn't imagine having to hold on to something so vile, nor could she imagine loving someone so much that she would do anything—including burning dead bodies and destroying missing people's belongings—to keep them. Sarah looked at Cavanaugh and wondered if she'd ever go to that extreme for him. The thought of what his parents had done made her want to vomit. She covered her mouth and coughed, sending a small spray of rancidness up into her nasal cavity. She grabbed a tissue, thinking of the other women Art had killed and wondered what had been so different about her. Why and how had she survived? She still couldn't remember anything about her "accident," grateful for the amnesia.

Sarah felt like a pendulum of ambivalence. She felt sorry for the elder Joneses, but also relief that she'd be safe from them, that no one else would endure what she had to or worse.

By the time Sarah tuned back in, she couldn't follow anything Cooley said. Besides that, he'd used a lot of police and legal jargon that she did not understand, though she hoped Cavanaugh did. Sarah had not been paying much attention until Pine offered a folded piece of paper to Cavanaugh.

"What's this?" he asked.

"It's a copy of a letter your mother wrote. We couldn't give you the original, but we thought it would do you well to have it."

"Thanks." Cavanaugh appeared to have a hard time getting the word out of his mouth.

"Well, we've got work to do, so we'll leave you two alone. Just thought it better to give you the news ourselves. We are sorry for your loss and everything you've been through," Cooley gave an earnest look to each Jones.

"That means a lot to us. Thank you so much...for everything," Sarah responded.

The officers exited the room and Cavanaugh held the letter for a long time before opening it. He looked at Sarah as he pulled at the folded paper. She returned his gaze, her eyes sad and face flushed as if she'd flood the room with tears at any moment. When Cavanaugh unfolded the paper, a smaller sheet slipped from between its folds onto his lap. He didn't seem to notice, but Sarah did. Evidence of the weathered page from which the letter had been copied, showed at the edges of the fresh, white copy paper. Sarah watched as Cavanaugh looked at the letter, waiting for him to begin reading. She saw his eyes make zig-zags across the sheet and down to the bottom, then he looked to her.

"Would you mind?" he asked. Sarah pushed herself up out of the chair. "Reading it to me, I mean?" He handed Sarah the letter.

Without a word, Sarah took the page from his trembling fingers, reseated herself and wiped at her eyes before she began to read the words aloud. Once she'd finished, she read them again after Cavanaugh prompted her to.

In the letter, Cynthia explained some things and apologized for others in an emotion-laden display of the words she'd never spoken. Cavanaugh just sat there. He didn't move or speak. He just stared straight ahead as Sarah's voice carried the words to his eardrums. After the second read, Sarah reached into Cavanaugh's lap and picked up the sheet that had fallen out. To her surprise, her name had been written on the surface. She opened it and read those words aloud as well.

Sarah,

You are a Jones. I admit that I've been quite leery of you, especially when you first arrived, but I have grown fond of you. I know this is late in coming and I should have told you long before now, but I was afraid. Afraid to get attached to you, to love you. Afraid that you were only passing through and more afraid to have you ripped away from me. I never had a daughter. What woman doesn't dream of having one? I was unable to conceive after CJ was born and I refused to try when I discovered Art's illness. I couldn't risk him hurting our child. I don't know what exempted CJ or myself from the danger of Art and his sickness. Sadly, I can't say the same for you. I thought you were safe, would be safe since he loved you so...and he did love you, Sarah. So did I. I am so sorry for what you've had to endure because of our secrets. The truth is, I'm relieved. I am so thankful that this is all over. No more secrets, no more danger, no more hiding. I will have to atone for my actions, my sins. Art has paid the heaviest price for his, but know that I am not angry with you. Shoulder no blame for saving my son, for you are braver than I am.

Cynthia

By the time Sarah got to the end of the letter, she was sobbing. Cavanaugh's eyes were lined with tears, the whites having turned red. He had lost both his parents in the most unimaginable way. He never had any clue his father had been so ill. Of course, the man acted strange at times but who didn't think their parents were a little strange? To his own surprise, Cavanaugh harbored no resentment or anger towards either of his parents. His father wasn't in control of his own mind, and though his actions were inexcusable, Cavanaugh felt compassion for him. Regarding Cynthia, in a weird way, he understood his mother's love for Art and the impossible lengths she went to because of it. Now that he knew love first hand, the kind of love his parents had for one another, it somehow made it easier to comprehend.

EPILOGUE

The California sun streaked across their naked bodies, the window blinds making symmetrical lines of light and shade. Sarah's hair, now past her shoulders, lay across the pillow, her usual blond reduced down to just the tips. Strands of her hair tickled Cavanaugh's armpit as she lay upon his chest.

"Mrs. Jones," Cavanaugh sang, although he hadn't opened his eyes yet.

"Hmm?" Sarah hummed, rolling onto her side and throwing an arm over her eyes to block out the sunlight.

"Wake up."

"You wake up!" she grumbled.

"But it's your wedding day." He nudged her with his knee.

"It's yours too. You asked for this, not me." She jabbed him with her elbow.

"Ugh," he grunted.

"Come to think of it, the first one was your idea too."

"You know you wanted a wedding. Every girl does."

"Not more than you, girlie-man!" She laughed and he chuckled. "I told you I was happy just being married to you. I didn't need an actual wedding."

Sarah rolled over onto her back, keeping her eyes closed against the brilliant yellow light.

"Well, it's too late now. Everyone's here and there's a wedding happening right outside. You're not going to leave me at the altar are you?"

"Yep! I sure am. I'll be right here, napping. Just recite your vows and mine. No one will know the difference."

"So, what you're saying is, you want me to go and marry myself?"

"That's a great idea! Let's do that!" Sarah giggled.

By now, the two of them had opened their eyes, but lay in each other's arms as if they had nothing to do and nowhere to go. They stayed that way for about an hour, debating whose idea it had been to have a California wedding.

Not long after Cynthia's trial, Cavanaugh and Sarah relocated to Napa Valley, California. Their new lives in Napa resembled their lives in San Antonio but with some key modifications. Cavanaugh had become a lot more responsible, now managing and running the entire family business, carrying on where Art and Cynthia had left off. He and Sarah bought a ranch about half the size of the estate back in Texas but with enough land to have a barn, horses, and an obstacle course so Sarah could finally train as a jumper. They also had a pool on the property and a guesthouse where Sarah's father and Cavanaugh's best friend, Neil, were staying for a few days. Taylor-Lynn, who'd also come in town for the wedding, slept in a room down the hall. Other friends and family had flown in as well and were, perchance, in transit while Cavanaugh and Sarah still lay in bed.

"Knock, knock," Taylor-Lynn's voice slipped through the crack under their bedroom door as she said knock, knock, instead of actually knocking.

"Just a sec," Sarah answered after a moment of muted giggles. She buried her face in Cavanaugh's neck as she contemplated not saying anything at all.

Sarah tried to slide out of bed, but Cavanaugh pulled her on top of him, laughing aloud as he tickled and kissed her. She writhed, pretending she wanted to get to the door when they both knew she didn't.

"See, if you didn't have a wedding to go to, we could stay in bed just like this." Sarah teased her husband by wiggling on top of him.

"Mmm," he groaned in tortured pleasure.

"I'll come back," Taylor-Lynn said from the other side of the door. Sarah heard her trying to stifle a giggle of her own.

"No, I'm just, uh...I'll be right there!" Sarah pulled away from Cavanaugh, grabbing her purple satin robe and slipping into it.

"You cruel, cruel woman, you."

She threw Cavanaugh a sly smile and opened the door just enough to slither through a small slot.

Less than an hour later she, Cavanaugh, and some friends and family, including Henrietta, were all gathered on a cliff, overlooking a nearby vineyard. This time the couple wed in public—no secrets, no hiding.

Not much about their ceremony was traditional. Sarah didn't walk down the aisle nor did she have any bridesmaids. She didn't wear the garb of a customary bride, instead, choosing to don a short lavender-colored dress, ruffled at the hem and paired with her favorite cowgirl boots. Cavanaugh dressed the way he did every day: jeans, boots and blazer and Sarah didn't mind at all. The ceremony lasted a mere twelve minutes. When the time came for Sarah to put the ring on Cavanaugh's finger, she slid on the mood ring he'd worn since their first set of nuptials, the biggest smile on her face. Once her turn came, she giggled as Cavanaugh dug in the pocket of his blazer for her matching mood ring. A few seconds ticked by and Cavanaugh still searched.

"Hurry up, will ya?" Sarah teased.

Cavanaugh looked at Neil, who stood before them, officiating their union for the second time.

"Don't look at me, man. I don't have it!" Neil winked.

A few more pats of his pockets and Cavanaugh, at last, pulled out Sarah's ring. A collective sigh echoed from their attendees. Sarah couldn't see the ring pinched between his large fingers as he slipped it onto her finger. He placed his hand over hers, looked into her eyes and mouthed 'I love you.'

"I know," Sarah acknowledged aloud with a giggle.

Cavanaugh pulled his hand away, revealing a cushion cut, purple diamond ring with a platinum band.

"I told you I'd get you a real ring," he said with a sly, triumphant smile.

Sarah hadn't looked her hand, hadn't expected anything different from her original mood ring.

"What?" She gave him what's-the-big-deal look.

Cavanaugh nodded towards her hand.

With a confused expression, Sarah looked down, for no other reason than to find out what he'd meant. She gasped, staring at the ring for a long minute before looking up at Cavanaugh with tears in her eyes. The tears surprised her because she hadn't been emotional all day, at least not until now. Speechless, Sarah threw her arms around Cavanaugh's neck and crushed her lips to his.

"Ahem, I didn't say you could kiss," Neil reprimanded.

Neither paid attention to Neil or everyone's laughter behind them, continuing to kiss as if they weren't surrounded by people. It didn't look as though they'd tear away from each other anytime soon.

"I, once again, pronounce you man and wife," Neil announced. "Publicly," he mumbled under his breath. "You may now kiss your bride."

Neil rattled the words off, not as much for them but for their few guests. Everyone stood and cheered while

Sarah and Cavanaugh carried on with their affections.

Later that night, after a Texas-style barbecue pool party that doubled as a wedding reception, Cavanaugh awoke with a start. He sat up in bed, glad that he had not disturbed his not-so-new wife. He looked at her, leaned over, and pulled the curtain of hair from her face. She stirred, letting out a deep sigh. Sliding out of bed, he went to the restroom trying to shake off the visions from his nightmare, but they flickered in his head like a fast-moving slide show. Cavanaugh could see himself in the pool of Sarah's blood all over again. He could see his father standing over him with an arrow aimed to kill. He could see his father's body on the ground beside him. He hadn't told Sarah about his nightmares, his grim visions, or flashbacks.

At the basin, Cavanaugh splashed water on his face, hoping the gruesome pictures would spiral down the sink with the water and into the sewer where they belonged. He looked at his reflection in the mirror, watching the clear droplets drip from points on his face while holding on to either side of the sink. Just as it happened before, Cavanaugh saw the corner of his mouth tilt up into a tiny smile.

"No!" he said, the word sounding like a growl.

He backed away from the mirror, grabbed a towel, and scrubbed his face. He looked again, waiting for a sign that he'd seen what he thought he had, but he saw nothing out of the ordinary. Once again, he couldn't decide if he'd seen the smile or not. Cavanaugh threw the towel into the bowl of the sink and after one long look in the mirror, he walked away from his reflection.

He climbed back into bed and inched close to Sarah, pulling her into the curve of his body. She fit into him like a puzzle piece, measured and cut precisely for him. Cavanaugh placed his lips on the small scar between her shoulder blades and kissed it. She sighed again and wriggled closer to him while pulling his arm tight around her middle. He lay his head on the pillow and let out a sigh of his own before falling to sleep, a tiny smile tilting the corner of his mouth yet again.

Then you will call to me. You will
come and pray to me, and I will answer you.
Jeremiah 29:12

DSEANBOOKS.COM

Acknowledgements

Thanks to my friends who urged me to finish this book. Specifically, to Marquia for reading the pages before they were complete and for calling me everyday to make sure I'd added to the page count.